W9-BFL-255

SAJO AND THE BEAVER PEOPLE

SAJO AND
THE BEAVER PEOPLE

By
GREY OWL

WITH SKETCHES BY THE AUTHOR

MACMILLAN OF CANADA
TORONTO

Copyright © 1935 Grey Owl

All rights reserved. The use of any part of
this publication reproduced, transmitted in
any form or by any means, electronic,
mechanical, photocopying, recording, or
otherwise, or stored in a retrieval system,
without the prior consent of the publisher
is an infringement of copyright law.

First printed 1935
Reprinted 1935 (4 times), 1937 (twice), 1941,
1942 (twice), 1943, 1944, 1945, 1947, 1950,
1951, 1955, 1958, 1961, 1966, 1970, 1973

ISBN   0-7705-1104-X   Cloth
           0-7705-1105-8   Paper

Printed in Canada for
The Macmillan Company of Canada Limited
70 Bond Street
Toronto, Ontario M5B 1X3

TO

CHILDREN EVERYWHERE

AND TO ALL

WHO LOVE THE SILENT PLACES

CONTENTS

ILLUSTRATIONS

ix

x

INTRODUCTION TO THE NEW EDITION

This book is the make-believe story of two children and their love affair with two little beavers. Sajo, the girl, aged eleven, and her brother Shapian, fourteen, are Ojibway Indians living at the edge of wilderness in northeastern Canada in the 1920s. Their mother is dead. Their father saves the lives of the beaver kittens, which are then adopted into the family. When the father runs out of money, he is obliged to sell one of the pets to an agent for a private zoo in a faraway city. In seeking to recover the beaver, the children encounter a forest fire, run a perilous river by canoe, and have many other adventures in a land and a time which now seem remote but which are made very real.

Though the story is fiction, it is based on the true-life experience of the author, Grey Owl. As a canoeman, packer, guide, and furtrapper, he had wandered for years in eastern Canada. When he wrote about Sajo and the beavers, he had been married for ten years to Anahareo, an Indian woman. The couple had a daughter of their own and also had adopted a series of beavers that lived more or less intimately with the family, and that became famous through magazine articles, books, lectures, and motion pictures created in whole or in part by Grey Owl.

The man who, in middle life, adopted the Ojibway name *Wa-sha-quon-asin,* or Grey Owl, was an expert in covering his tracks, both in the wilderness and in his private career. The facts of his early life are obscure. According to a one-page biography by Norah Story in *The Oxford Companion to Canadian History and Literature,* he was George Stanfeld Belaney (1888-1938), born in Hastings, England, son of George Belaney and a woman of unknown antecedents from Florida. The British Museum, however, lists him as Archibald Stansfeld Belaney. According to Norah Story's biography, "Grey Owl claimed that his mother had Indian blood, but there seems to be good reason to doubt this; nevertheless he clung to what is now thought to be a childhood fantasy, came in time to believe that he was an Indian, and created a legend that deceived many people." In the preface to Grey Owl's first book, *The Men of the Last Frontier,* published in 1931, the editor explained that "the author is a half-breed Indian, whose name has recently become known throughout the English-speaking world. His father was a Scot, his mother an Apache Indian of New Mexico, and he was born somewhere near the Rio Grande forty odd years ago." So much for his origin; the extent to which he drifted in and out of Indian country, either truly or in imagination, is perhaps unimportant.

Grey Owl emigrated to Canada in 1903 at the age of fifteen. He returned to England to serve in the First World War, was wounded, and went back to Canada to live with the Ojibways in northern Ontario. The service pension of $15 a month that he received from the Canadian government kept him alive during the postwar economic depression, when he had given up trapping and was struggling to establish a beaver sanctuary. In 1926 he moved to northern Quebec with his Indian wife, Anahareo.

His creative years began in 1929, the year his first story on wildlife, "The Passing of the Last Frontier," was published in the English magazine *Country Life*. He began to lecture on conservation that year and in 1931 went to Alberta as an honorary ranger in the Canadian national parks system, first in Riding Mountain National Park and later in Prince Albert National Park, where he lived the rest of his life. Besides *The Men of the Last Frontier,* already mentioned, and *Sajo and the Beaver People,* which was first published in 1935, he was the author of *Pilgrims of the Wild* (1934) and *Tales from an Empty Cabin* (1936). French and German translations were also published during the height of his career.

The style of the present book may occasionally seem quaint to young readers of today. For example, Irishmen in real life are unlikely to speak the way the one in the story does: "I'm on dooty and cannot leave; but set ye down and wait, and I'll take ye there. And it's Patrick O'Reilly himself will see that no harm comes to yez" (page 137). But this aspect of the style is less important than the excitement of the story or the lively, poetic word-pictures by which Grey Owl describes the lives of the animals and the Indians who associate with them.

Though Grey Owl says in this Preface (page xvii) that his "delineations of animal character are to be taken as authentic," the skeptical reader will try to separate fact from poetry, enjoying each for its own sake. Biologists will cringe at the application of the words "evil," "cruel," and "sly" to the otter that breaks into the beaver lodge (page 25). Yet it is hard for people not to take sides with one wildlife species or against another. We see a weasel stalking a baby quail, and our first thought is to frighten the predator away. Only later do we consider that the weasel may

INTRODUCTION

have a hungry brood of young ones somewhere in a den depending for life on the food the mother brings them.

Professional biologists are trained to shun anthropomorphism —the attribution to animals of human motivation or characteristics—in recording wildlife behavior. For natural-history writers, or interpreters of such behavior, this restriction is less important. In the act of translation, the writer is called upon to explain the activities—and sometimes to interpret the thoughts—of the animal in terms intelligible to the general reader.

A mother who reads the story of *Sajo and the Beaver People* to a child can explain that animals are never "good" or "bad" in the human sense. By pointing out that all people are richer for sharing a world with animals and by discussing the wealth of the Indian cultures, she can use the simple tale of Sajo to open a door to unknown places and fresh ideas. Older children, reading the book for the sake of the story, will at the same time be introduced to some of these ideas, whether or not they are aware of the fact. And adults with an interest in wildlife and the wilderness will also enjoy this lively and moving tale.

VICTOR B. SCHEFFER

PREFACE

WHILE the events recorded in this modest tale did not, in all instances, occur in the chronological order here appointed them, all of them have taken place within my knowledge. Indeed, most of them are recorded from personal experience and from first-hand narrations by the participators themselves.

Save for a few of the details connected with the two children's visit to the city (regarding which I had only the impressions of two bewildered youngsters to work on, and further obscured by the passage of over a quarter of a century), no circumstances have been brought in that are not actual fact.

Any Indian words used are correctly rendered from the Ojibway language, in the regional dialect of the area involved, and are spelled phonetically so as to simplify pronunciation. The words are simple, and their meanings are made to appear in an easy and natural manner.

In the illustrations I have made no attempt at artistry, confining myself strictly to clear outlines, in the interests of accuracy—not that my efforts in this direction were at all endangered by any vigorous attacks of artistic ability. My two sole departures into the, to me, treacherous field of poetic license occur, firstly, in the head of the moose that is shown in Chapter II (facing page 10). Although the scene is laid in the month of May, I have given him a full set of antlers, as he would appear later in the season, thus offering a more interesting educational exhibit than would the somewhat mule-like creature he would appear without them. Secondly, the owl that is represented in Chapter IV (facing page 36) is not of the variety known as the Laughing Owl, who, in spite of his vocal capabilities, is rather a commonplace, uninteresting-looking specimen of his genus. I have therefore supplanted him by the more representative type, known as the Great Horned Owl. So, like all good transgressors whose misdeeds are about to be exposed, I make this timely confession.

The delineations of animal character are to be taken as authentic, and the mental and physical reactions ascribed to the animals are as nearly correct as a lifetime of intimate association with wild life, in its own environment, can make them. These portrayals, as well as all other descriptions, have been very carefully drawn, so that the young reader will not be transported into a world that is altogether make-believe, but may gain new and pleasing impressions that need not later be discarded as mere phantasy. My intention was to write a child's story that could be read, without loss of dignity, by grown-ups.

It is highly probable that Chilawee and Chikanee,* the two beaver kittens who are the heroes of the story, survived to a ripe old age in their home-pond, for not only was this colony, after these events, considered inviolate by the hunters in whose trapping-grounds they were, as well as by the entire community, but soon after their release the region for many miles around was included within the boundaries of a well-known Provincial Park. The Yellow Birch river—in fact the whole area—re-

* Pronounced *Chill*-a-wee and Chik-a-*nee*.

mains in very nearly the same unspoiled condition it was in at the time of the story. The name of the stream itself has been changed since old Indian days, though it may still be identified by those who chance to travel on its waters, by the magnificent forests of yellow birch, maple and other hardwoods that still clothe the granite hills through which it flows.

Gitchie Meegwon, or, in English, Big Feather, known as "Quill" to the white people who later entered the region, was a personal and well-loved friend of my younger days, and has long since joined the Great Majority. My first trap trail was laid under his highly efficient and somewhat stern direction. A bark canoe, made by this man, is still on exhibition at the Normal School museum on Church Street in Toronto, or was at the time of my last visit there in 1911. His character was such that I have taken the liberty of substituting him for the real father of Sajo and Shapian, who has also passed on. Sajo and Shapian have been beyond my ken this many years, so that to me they have never grown up, and are still the very winning little girl and the tall, serious-minded, courageous lad that they were in those dear dead days that are gone. The town to which they made their adventurous pilgrimage was not, at that time, the vast metropolis it seemed to them, and although it did not for a long time attain to that distinction, I have, in this narrative, made use of a privilege accorded to the Tellers of the Tales, not only among our people but the world over, and present it as it appeared in their eyes, dignifying it with the title of "The City."

It is my hope that, besides providing an hour or two of entertainment, this simple story of two Indian children and their well-loved animal friends may awaken in some eager, inquiring young minds a clearer and more intimate understanding of the joys and the sorrows, the work, the pastimes and the daily lives of the humble little People of the forest, who can experience feelings so very like their own. And the writer even ventures, at the risk of being considered presumptuous, to allow himself the thought that perhaps, too, it may invoke in the hearts of even those of more mature years a greater tolerance and sympathy for those who are weaker or less gifted than themselves.

Above all, may it be my privilege to carry with me, as fellow-voyagers on this short, imaginary journey to the Northland, a small but happy company of those who, for so short a time, dwell in that Enchanted Vale of Golden Dreams that we call Childhood.

GREY OWL (WA-SHA-QUON-ASIN)

BEAVER LODGE

PRINCE ALBERT NATIONAL PARK,
SASKATCHEWAN, CANADA

SAJO AND THE BEAVER PEOPLE

I

The Land of the North-West Wind

FAR, far away beyond the cities, the towns and the farmlands that you are so used to seeing all about you, away beyond the settlements of Northern Canada, lies a wild, almost unknown country. If you wished to see it you would have to journey over the hills and far away, to where there are neither railways nor roads, nor houses nor even paths, and at last you would have to travel in a canoe with your Indian guides, through a great, lonely land of forest, lake and river, where moose, deer, bears and wolves roam free, and where sometimes great herds of caribou wander across the country in such vast numbers that no one could possibly count them, even if he were there to do so.

Here, in this great Northland, you would see a part of North America as it was before the white man discovered it, and as it will remain, I hope, for many, many years to come. You would not see very many white people there, even today, for besides the few trappers and traders, the only human beings that live there are the scattered bands of Ojibway* Indians that have made this land their home, calling it the Land of Keewaydin,† the North-west wind. They are a race of people so ancient, and they have been there so long, that no one, not

* Pronounced O-*jib*-way.   † Pronounced Kee-*way*-din.

even they themselves, know where they came from or how they ever got there. Far beyond the reach of civilization, they live very much as their forefathers did when Jacques Cartier landed on these shores over four hundred years ago. Their villages of teepees,* tents and sometimes log cabins, are still to be found, often a hundred miles apart, in sheltered groves and sunny openings in the woods, or beside the sandy beaches on some pleasant lake shore. In these small towns the Indian families live, each in its own dwelling, in happiness and contentment, well-fed in good times, going a little hungry when times are bad, as is the case with more civilized people.

Everybody in these villages has work to do; even the young people must do their share. Nearly all this work has to do with travelling, as Indians are constantly on the move. Some seasons, the animals on which the Indians depend for a living disappear out of a district, and the people must follow them or find new hunting-grounds, so that whole villages have to be pulled down, and everything (except the log cabins, of course,) must be loaded in canoes or on toboggans, according to the time of year, and moved for many miles. On these Winter trips little boys and girls take their turn at breaking trail on snow-shoes, feeling very proud as they lead the long procession of dog-teams and toboggans and people, for a mile or two at a time. In Summer they paddle all day in the canoes with the older people, and each has his or her small load to carry on the portages. They really enjoy their work, and they are just as serious and business-like about their tasks as are their parents.

*Pronounced *tee*-pee.

"THESE SMALL TOWNS THE INDIANS LIVE, BESIDE SOME PLEASANT LAKE SHORE"

Those of the Indian children who spend their summers near a fur-post or on a reservation, have an opportunity to go to school, and often make good scholars; some, indeed, become lawyers, others doctors, writers, or artists, and are very successful. But those of them who live the year round in the wild country have an education of another kind. The forest is their school, and in it they study the lessons so necessary to their way of life. Geography, history, or arithmetic or English would be of no use to them; their studies are plant and tree life, the ways and habits of animals and how to track them; how to catch fish at all times of the year and, most important of all, how to make fire in any kind of weather, such as rain, wind or snow. They learn the calls of all the birds and beasts, and can imitate some of them very well. They are trained to observe the movements of water in the rivers and lakes, so as to become skilful in the handling of canoes, and they learn the proper use of snow-shoes, guns and axes, and how to drive a dog-team besides such every-day tasks as sewing moccasins, tanning hides, and finding firewood in places where there looks to be none at all; and they must be able to cook. Such a thing as a compass is unknown to them, and they can travel anywhere they wish in the forest by means of the sun, stars, moon, shapes of trees, formation of the hills, movements of animals and many other signs far too numerous to mention here. Their knowledge of woodcraft is so great that they become very self-reliant, and are able to make long trips alone and face without fear many dangers, as did the Indian boy and girl in this story.

The Indian life is so hard and toilsome that no one in these villages can be lazy very long without quickly running short of food, clothing or shelter; and while the people will help one another and divide up whatever they may have, a lazy person is very much looked down on. Yet in spite of all this hard work, the younger people find much time to play their simple and very active games. Sometimes, after the day is done and darkness falls, they will sit out beneath the glittering northern stars, around the blazing camp-fires, and listen to the tales of their elders. Some of these tales are about hunting trips, or far-off tribes of Indians, or about great men of long ago; others are about strange adventures in the forest. But the strangest tales of all, to them, are told by those of the grown-ups who have visited that wonderful country so far away to the south, where the white people come from; where are great sleighs on wheels that run with the speed of wind over an iron trail, by which they mean the railroad, and where smoke-canoes, as they call steamboats, go nearly as fast on the water; where there are no Indians and not many trees, only rows of tall stone houses between which people walk in crowds, rushing, hurrying along, seeming to go nowhere and come from nowhere. A country, they are told, where if you have no money you cannot sleep or eat. And they find this last to be the very strangest thing of all, because in the woods travellers are always welcome to rest and eat in the camps of white trappers or in an Indian village, free of any charge. For these children, and most of the older people too, know as little about the necessities of city life as perhaps you do about their wilderness.

And now, as chance travellers from the distant settlements

tell to these black-eyed, smiling Indian children stories of a land they have never seen, so I, who once was one of them, will tell to you a tale from that great wilderness that is so far away.

First, though, you must know that all through this forest that is so dark and mysterious, with its strange animals and people, there run a great many rivers, which are used as highways not only by the Indians in their swift canoes, but by many water beasts such as beaver, otter, mink and muskrats. And in the woods are countless trails, although perhaps you could never find them, on which the animals that live on land travel as though upon a road. For all these creatures are continually on the move. They, as well as the humans in this land, are always busy. They have their living to find or make, and their young ones to take care of and feed. Some live alone, with no settled home, and others keep together in large numbers, having good-sized towns tunnelled out beneath the ground, the different houses of each family joined, in groups, by passages. The very wisest among them, such as beaver, build themselves warm houses, store up water in which to swim, and put up large supplies of food for the winter months, working almost like men, often talking together when resting from their labours; and they all have, each in their own way, a great deal to attend to.

And on account of their cleverness and industry, the Indians, even though they must kill some of them in order to make a living, cannot help but respect these animals and take a great interest in all they do, looking on them almost as separate tribes of people, of a kind little different from themselves. Beavers are especially respected, and some Indians can understand to a certain extent what they are saying to one another, as their voices are not unlike those of human beings. All animals, however small or apparently useless, have their own proper place, and the Indians know this, and never bother them without good reason; and because they share with them the hardships of this forest life, they call them Little Brothers. Frequently they keep them as pets, and you will often see bear cubs, young beavers or perhaps an otter, or sometimes a calf moose or a deer running loose in an Indian encampment, free to go wherever they want, but staying around just because they feel at home and seem to enjoy the bustle and excitement of camp life. As they become full-grown, so they eventually wander away, but it is not for long that the village will be without pets of some kind or another.

And now that you know what the country is like and how the Indians live, and have heard a little about some of the animals, I will tell you a tale of the Little People of the Forest, a tale that is real, and has its beginning on one of those waterways I told you of, where lived a happy family of the Beaver People.

I will tell you about an Indian hunter and his young son and daughter, and of two small kitten beavers that were their friends. And you shall hear of their adventures in the great forests of the North, and in the city too; of what good chums they were, and how one of them was lost and found again, and about the dangers they were in and all the fun they had, and what came of it all.

And now we will clean forget the motor-cars, the radio and

the movies and all the things we thought we could not do without, and we'll think instead of dog-teams, of canoes and tents and snow-shoes, and we'll journey to that far-off, magic land.

And there you'll see great rivers, and lakes and whispering forests, and strange animals that talk and work, and live in towns; where the tall trees seem to nod to you and beckon as you pass them, and you hear soft singing voices in the streams.

And we'll sit beside a flickering camp-fire in a smoky, dark-brown wigwam, while you listen to this tale of Long Ago.

II

GITCHIE MEE–GWON, THE BIG FEATHER

U P the broad, swift current of the Yellow Birch river, in the days before the eyes of a white man had ever looked on its cool, clear waters, there paddled one early September morning a lone Indian in a birch-bark canoe. He was a tall, gracefully built man with keen dark eyes, and long black hair that fell in two braids over his shoulders. He was dressed in a suit of fringed buckskin that had been smoked to a rich brown, and altogether he looked a good deal like those Indians you see in pictures, or read about.

His canoe was bright yellow, dyed with the juice of alders to the same colour as the stout, golden-tinted trunks of the yellow birch trees that covered the surrounding hills, and the seams along its sides were sealed with narrow strips of shiny, black spruce-gum, to keep the water out. This canoe had a large eye, like that of some enormous bird, painted on the front of it, and behind, at the very end, was fastened the tail of a fox, which swayed gently back and forth in the breeze. For the Indian liked to feel that his canoe was actually alive and had a head and a tail like all the other creatures, and was sharp-eyed like a bird, and swift and light like a fox. In it there was a neatly folded tent, a small bag of provisions, an axe, a tea-pail, and a long, old-fashioned rifle.

From the tops of the birches on the hill-sides there came a low whispering, a sound of rustling that never seemed to cease, as the wind played amongst the leaves, so that the Indians had named these highlands the Hills of the Whispering Leaves. The river banks were lined by a forest of tall, dark pine trees, and their huge limbs hung out over the water, far above it; and along the shore beneath them robins, blackbirds, and canaries flew and fluttered, searching for their breakfast among the new grasses and the budding leaves of the pussy willows. The air was heavy with the sweet smell of sage and wild roses, and here and there a hummingbird shot like a brilliant purple arrow from one blossom to another. For this was May, called by the Indians the Month of Flowers.

Gitchie Meegwon,* the Big Feather, for such was the Indian's name, belonged to the Ojibway† nation. He had paddled against the strong current of the Yellow Birch river for many days, and was now far from his village. Steadily, day after day, he had forged ahead, sometimes moving along easily on smooth water as he was doing now, at other times poling up rough rapids, forcing his frail canoe up the rushing, foaming water and between jagged, dangerous rocks with a skill that few white men and not all Indians learn. This morning his way was barred by a waterfall, wild and beautiful, higher than the tallest pine trees, where the sun made a rainbow in the dashing white spray at the foot of it. Here he landed, just beyond the reach of the angry, hungry-looking whirlpool that tried very hard to pull his canoe in under the thundering falls. Picking up the canoe

---

* Pronounced *Git*-chie *Mee*-gwon.　　† Pronounced O-*jib*-way.

he carried it, upside down on his shoulders, over a dim portage trail between the giant whispering trees, a trail hundreds of years old, and on which the sun never shone, so shaded was it. He made a second trip with his light outfit, loaded his canoe, and out in the brightness and the calm water above the falls, continued his journey.

He glanced sharply about, as the bends in the river opened up before him, and saw many things that would have escaped the eyes of any one but a hunter; an exciting glimpse of a pair of furry ears pointed his way, the rest of the creature hidden; or of bright eyes that gleamed out at him from the shadows. Once he saw a silver-coated lynx fade like a grey shadow into the underbrush. Here and there deer leaped hastily away towards the woods, whistling loudly through their nostrils as they bounded like red rocking-horses through the forest, their tails flashing like white, swaying banners between the trees. Once he came upon a great moose, as big as any horse, who stood chest-deep in the river, his head buried under the surface while he dug for lily roots on the bottom. As Big Feather paused to look at the moose who, busy with his task, had not heard him, the huge creature raised his head with a mighty splurge and stood there staring in surprise, while the water poured in streams from his face and neck. Then he turned and plunged ashore and soon was gone, though the heavy thudding of his hoofs and the sharp crack of breaking limbs and small trees could still be heard for a minute or two as he galloped crashing through the woods.

Even with all this company, Gitchie Meegwon was a little

"ONCE HE SAW A SILVER-COATED LYNX"

lonely, for back at the village, now so far away, he had left his two young children, a girl and a boy. Their mother had died, and while the women of the village were kind to them, they missed their mother very much, and he knew they must be lonesome too, as he was. The three of them were great friends and were seldom parted, and every place he went their father always took them. But this time he was alone, as this was likely to be a dangerous journey, for he expected to have trouble with some poachers before it was finished. Gitchie Meegwon had built a fine log cabin for his small family, for a Summer home, and there they had been happy and comfortable together, resting after the hard Winter's hunt, when word had been brought in by a friendly Cree Indian that a band of half-breeds from down near the settled country had invaded the region, and were killing all the beaver as they went through it in large parties. The real bush Indians do not hunt on each other's trapping grounds, considering such behaviour to be stealing, but these town-bred half-breeds had given up or forgotten the old ways, and were likely to clean out every trapping ground as they came to it. And without fur with which to buy provisions at the trading post, Big Feather's family would go hungry. So now he was up here, deep into his Winter hunting ground, to protect it from these strangers. But he had seen none of them nor any sign of them, and the weather being now warm, and fur-animals no longer worth stealing, he felt that his work was done, and tomorrow he intended to turn back for home.

With these pleasant thoughts in mind, he was passing along close to the river bank, watching for any tracks there might be left by the careless half-breeds, when all at once he smelt a strong, sharp scent upon the air—some beast, or perhaps a man, had passed nearby and crushed the spicy-smelling leaves of a mint plant. Instantly on the alert, he glanced quickly at the bank, when suddenly a short, dark, heavily built animal sprang out into the river right in front of his canoe and sank like a stone, out of sight. Almost immediately a black head and a brown, furry back came floating up a short distance away, and the creature swam rapidly round the canoe until, cleverly getting to a spot where the wind was from the Indian to himself, he caught the man-scent, that all the Forest People fear so much. Down came his wide, flat tail on the water with a terrific splash, the water flying in all directions as he dived like a flash, this time for good.

Big Feather shook a few drops from the sleeve of his leather shirt, and smiled; this was very much what he had wanted to see. It had been a beaver. And before the echo of the beaver's alarm signal had died away, there came another from around the next bend, sharp and loud, almost like a gun-shot. There were two of them.

The Indian smiled again, for now he began to feel sure that no one had hunted here. These beaver would have been only too easy to catch; if these careless fellows, who allowed him to get so close to them, right on a main highway so to speak, had not been captured, the rest of them must all be safe. Still, to make certain, he decided to visit their home, where there should be others. Their house would not be hard to find as beaver, when on their travels, cut small green saplings of alder, poplar, and willow here and there, eating the bark off them, and these peeled sticks show white and shiny every place they land, so a person has only to follow from one to another of these feeding places, to discover where they live. Very soon the Indian came to where a little stream ran down into the river, and at its mouth he found what he expected, a number of these slim, shining sticks, remains of a beaver's meal. No doubt their house would be somewhere up the little stream, in some quiet spot such as beavers love.

The beavers had eaten at the edge of a nice open point where a few giant pine trees stood about, as though they had wandered out from the forest and could not get back again. Here Gitchie Meegwon made a small fire and had his own noon meal. Indians drink a good deal of tea on their travels, so leaning a slim pole over the cheerful blaze he hung his tea-pail on one end of it to boil, the other end being stuck firmly into the ground to hold it in position; he arranged strips of deer-meat on sharp forked sticks, before the hot coals, and under them placed slices of Indian bread, or bannock as it is called, to catch the delicious gravy that fell from the meat as it cooked. After he had eaten he smoked quietly for a little time, listening to the humming of the breeze in the wide, fan-shaped boughs of the pines. Very like music it sounded to him, as he leaned back contentedly and watched the lazy smoke wafting this way and that, as it made strange patterns in the air. For these things were his pictures and his music, all he ever had, and he enjoyed them perhaps as much as you do your movies and your radio.

Soon, after covering his small outfit with the overturned

canoe, he took his long-barrelled trade-gun and started up beside the brook, on his way to the beaver pond that he knew must be at the head of it. His moccasins made no sound, and left no track, as he walked softly in the quietness and calm of the sleepy forest, while squirrels shrilled and chattered at him from the boughs, and whiskey jacks, those knowing, cheerful camp birds to be seen nearly everywhere in the woods, followed him from tree to tree, sometimes getting ahead of him to peer wisely and whistle at him as he passed. He enjoyed the company these small creatures gave to him, and took his time and walked quite leisurely along. Suddenly he stopped, listening. His keen ears had caught a strange, unexpected sound, which quickly became louder and louder and was all at once a roar—and then he saw, coming swiftly down the creek bed towards him, a rush of yellow, muddy water, bringing with it a mass of sticks and litter which filled the banks to the very top and went pouring by in a wild, swirling torrent. Something terrible was happening up at the beaver pond! It could be only one thing; some man or beast, something, must have torn out the beaver dam, and this rushing torrent was the beavers' so carefully saved up water, without which they would be helpless.

In a moment, rifle in hand, Big Feather was leaping and tearing his way through the forest that had but a moment before been so pleasant, and seemed now so dark and threatening. Forward he raced at top speed, running on swift-moccasined feet to save his beaver colony from destruction, springing high over logs, smashing his way through windfalls and branches and tangled underbrush, leaving the squirrels and the camp birds far behind him, bounding like a deer through the shadowy woods towards the pond, hoping he would be in time. Well did he know what had happened.

Negik, the otter, bitter and deadly enemy of all the Beaver People, was on the war-path and the beavers, their water gone, must even now be fighting for their lives.

III

The Home of the Beaver People

H<small>AD</small> we walked up beside that bustling little creek while
Gitchie Meegwon was making his dinner, instead of
waiting to watch him as we did, we would have arrived at the
beavers' home before the otter broke the dam, and have seen
what it was like up there and how the beavers lived. We
would, after a rather long walk, have come out quite suddenly
on the shore of a small, deep pond. Right across the front of
this pond, and blocking the bed of the stream that came out
of it, was a thick, high wall of sticks and brush. It was all
very tightly woven, and the chinks were filled with moss and
the whole business well cemented with mud. Along the top
of it a number of heavy stones had been placed to keep it solid.
It was nearly one hundred feet long and more than four feet
high, and the water flowed over the top of it through a narrow
trough of sticks, so that the stream was wearing away at it in
only this one spot, where it could be easily controlled. So
well had it been made that it looked exactly as if a gang of
men had been working at it—but it was animals, not men,
that had built it.

This wall, which was really a dam, seemed as if it were
holding the lake in place: which is really what it was doing,
for without it there would have been no lake at all, only the
stream running through.

The pond was bright with sunshine; very silent and peaceful it was, back there among the Hills of the Whispering Leaves, and so calm that the few ducks dozing quietly upon its waters seemed almost to be floating on air, and the slim white poplar trees that stood upon its banks were reflected so plainly on its smooth surface, that it was hard to tell where the water stopped and the trees began. It was very beautiful, like a fairy-land, with its silver poplars and Mayflowers and blue water. And it was very still, for nothing moved there, and it seemed quite lifeless except for the sleeping ducks. Yet, had you watched patiently for a little while, being careful not to move or talk, or even whisper, you would have seen, before very long, a ripple on the water near the shore as a dark brown head, with round ears that showed very plainly, peered cautiously out from the rushes at the water's edge, and watched and listened and sniffed. The head was followed by a furry body, as its owner now came out in full sight and swam rapidly, but without a sound, to another place on the far shore, there to disappear among the reeds. The tall reeds swayed and shook for a minute as he worked there, and then he reappeared, this time holding before him a large bundle of grass, and swam over towards an enormous black mound of earth that we had been wondering about all this time, and dived, bundle and all, right in front of it. He had scarcely disappeared before another head, with another bundle, could be seen swimming from a different direction when—somebody moved, and with no warning at all, a huge flat tail came down on the water with a heavy smack, and with a mighty splash and a plunge the head and its bundle were gone. Now this was exactly what had happened to Big Feather, down on the river that morning, and for the same reason. For that great mound, taller than any of us, before which the swimmers had dived, was a beaver house, and the dark-brown, furry heads were those of the Beaver People themselves. And they had been very busy.

The lodge had been built up to more than six feet in height, and was a good ten feet across. It had lately been well plastered with wet mud, and heavy billets of wood had been laid on the slopes of it to hold everything firmly in place. It all looked very strong and safe, like a fortress, and even a moose could have walked around on top of it without doing it a bit of harm. Up the side of it there was a wide pathway, on which the building materials were carried, and had you been more patient or careful a while ago, or perhaps had the wind not played a trick on you and given you away to those keen noses, you might have seen old father beaver dig out a load of earth from the shore, go with it to the house, swimming slowly and carefully so as not to lose any, and then standing upright like a man, walk to the top of the roof with the load in his arms and there dump it, pushing it into nooks and crannies with his hands, and shoving a good-sized stick in after it to keep it there.

And all this work had been done with a purpose. It was a very important time, this Month of Flowers, for inside that queer-looking home, hidden away from the eyes of all the world, were four tiny kitten beavers. Woolly little fellows they were, perfectly formed, with bright black eyes, big webbed hind feet, little hand-like fore-paws and tiny, flat, rubbery-looking tails. They had marvellous appetites, and their lungs must have been very good too, for they were the noisiest little creatures imaginable and cried continuously in long, loud wails that were very much like the cries of small human babies. Like any other babies, they needed a great deal of attention—and you may be sure that they were getting a lot of it too.

The living room, or chamber, inside the lodge, was large enough for a person to have curled up in it with ease, and was very clean and sweet smelling with its floor of willow bark and bed of scented grasses. The entrance was through a short, slanting tunnel one end of which, called the plunge-hole, was in the floor, and the other end came out below, near the bottom of the lake. The dam held the pond up to a level nearly even with the floor, keeping the plunge-hole always full, so that the tiny kittens, who were a little wobbly on their legs as yet, could drink there without falling into it; or if they did (which happened rather regularly), they could climb out again quite easily. The whole tunnel and the outer doorway were under water, so that no land animals could enter, or even see it, unless they were first-class divers, which most of them are not. But if the dam should break and let the saved-up water out, the beaver would be in grave danger, as not only could their enemies, such as wolves and foxes, find their way into the house, but the beaver would be unable to protect or hide themselves by diving suddenly out of sight, as you saw them do a little while ago.

KEY TO DIAGRAM OF BEAVER WORKS

(*A.I. A.I.*) Beaver house. (*A.*2.) Interior of beaver house. The living room, or chamber. (*B.*) Sleeping platform. (*C.*) Lower level for drying off, draining into plunge-hole, at D. (*D*.) Plunge-hole. (*E.E.*) Tunnel leading out into deep water. (*F*.) Side, or emergency entrance, also used in discarding old bedding and used sticks. (*G*.) Main entrance. (*H.H.*) The dam. (*K*.) Spillway, for regulating overflow, and maintaining correct water level. (*L. L. & L. I.*) Trees felled, and partly felled by beaver. (*M.M.*) Bottom of pond. (*P.P.*) Feed raft. Greatest portion under water, below the reach of ice. (*S.S.*) Beaver runway, or hauling trail, used for removing required portions of tree, cut down by beavers, and marked *L.I.* (*W.W.*) Original stream resuming its course. (*Y*.) Stream running into pond, passing out at *K*. (*X.X.*) Bottom of pond has been dug out below the feed raft and in front of the dam, so as to obtain a greater depth of water. The materials thus obtained are used in the construction of the dam and house. (*Z. Z.*) Former dry land, now under water on account of dam. Without the dam there would be no pond, only the stream.

REMARKS

The house may be built close to the dam, but is often a considerable distance from it.

Note that the water level is exactly even with the plunge-hole.

Note that the swimming beavers have their front paws tucked up against their chests. The hind feet only are used in swimming, the front paws being used as hands, for working and picking up objects, or as feet for walking. Beavers do a considerable amount of walking on their hind feet, marching along slowly but very steadily; all loads consisting of earth, mud, or other loose materials, are carried in the arms, the beavers walking upright, like a man. The heavier sticks are drawn by means of the teeth, on all fours.

Beavers never use their tails for working in any way, except as a support in walking erect, or as a balancing-pole when clambering amongst fallen trees. In the water the tail is used as a rudder, sometimes as an oar, and for signalling by splashing on the water. This slapping sound is varied slightly, according to whether it is intended for an alarm signal, or as an indication of the owner's whereabouts. The kittens sometimes take a ride on their parents' tails.

If you look at the sketch, facing this page, you can see how it was all arranged, and will be able to realize how very important

PLAN OF BEAVER POND.

this dam was, and why the father spent so much of his time watching it and fixing any small leaks that appeared. He had, too, a pretty steady job keeping the trough, which you might call a regulator, clear of rubbish, so that the water could flow freely and not become too high, and so flood the house, but was always at exactly the right level. Between whiles, both he and the mother attended to their babies' every want, changing their bedding every so often, bringing in small sprays of tender leaves for them to eat, combing and brushing their wool (you could hardly call it fur), while they made queer, soft sounds of affection and talked to them in that strange beaver language that, at a little distance, sounds almost as though human people were speaking together in low voices. And the shrill wailing cries of the little ones, and their chattering, and their little squawks and squeals, could be heard even through the thick walls of the lodge, so noisy were they when they were hungry, or pleased, or in some small trouble, which, one way and another, was pretty nearly all the time. And when either their father or their mother returned (they were never away together; one or the other was always on guard) from a trip to the so-important dam, or brought in new bedding of sweet-grass, he or she would give a low, crooning sound of greeting, to be immediately answered by a very bedlam of loud shouts of welcome from the youngsters, that went on long after it was at all necessary. They were never still unless they were asleep, and were continually scrambling around, and tussling together, and clambering over everything, and by the noise they made, seemed to be enjoying themselves immensely. And altogether they were pretty much like any other family, and were very snug and happy in their home.

The little ones were now old enough to try their hand at swimming in the plunge-hole, though at present this exercise consisted mostly in lying on top of the water, not always right side up, and going round and round in circles, screeching with excitement. And being so very light, and their fluffy coats containing so much air, they could not seem to sink deep enough for their webbed hind feet to both get a grip on the water at the same time, so they swam with first one foot and then the other, rolling from side to side and bobbing up and down, squirming and squealing and wiggling, while their parents passed anxiously around amongst them, giving them encouragement, or perhaps advice, in their deep, strong voices. From what I have seen of such goings on, it must have been rather a troublesome time for the old folks, this business of learning to swim, but the youngsters seemed to be having a good time which, as you will agree, is, after all, something to be considered.

But they would soon become tired, and climbing out onto the drying-off place (a little lower than the rest of the floor, so the water would soak away and not run all over the beds), every little beaver carefully squeezed, rubbed and scrubbed the water from his coat on the front, sides, back, every place he could reach, sitting upright and working very industriously, puffing and blowing as most of us do after a swim. Then, when this was all over and everybody was dry, or thought he was (some of them would topple over once in a while and made rather a poor job of it), the call for lunch would go up in a loud chorus,

A PEEP INSIDE THE HOME OF THE BEAVER PEOPLE.

"THEIR FATHER AND MOTHER TOOK TURNS TO BRING IN BUNDLES OF SWEET-GRASS AND SPRAYS OF TENDER LEAFLETS."

G.O.

and the new green leaflets and water plants that had been provided ahead of time, with the idea, no doubt, of putting a stop to the uproar as soon as possible, would be divided up, and pretty soon all the busy little jaws would be munching away, and the piercing cries died down to mumbles and little mutterings of contentment. And soon the little voices became quiet and the small black eyes closed, while they lay cuddled together on their sweet-smelling, grassy bed, with their tiny fore-paws so much like hands, clutched tightly in each other's fur.

And this would be their daily program until, after perhaps three weeks, would come that glorious day when they would venture down the long, dim tunnel out into the brightness of the great unknown world that was all about them, but which they had never seen. And while they slept the old ones stood watch and guard, turn about, and took turns to inspect the defences of their castle and the dam on which their very lives depended, and kept a weather eye out for enemies, and collected food and bedding for when the babies should awaken, and carried on at the hundred and one jobs that make father and mother beaver a very busy pair of people during the latter part of May, the Moon of Flowers.

Our four young heroes, or heroines, or both, had just arrived at that thrilling stage of the proceedings when they could at last dive without bobbing up immediately, tail first, like a rubber ball, and could swim around on the surface for quite a respectable distance without calling loudly for help, when one day at noon, at the very time when we had been watching Gitchie Meegwon at his dinner, the father noticed that the water in the entrance was sinking. He watched it for a moment; the mother heard it too, heard it gurgling and came to look—the water was going down, swirling down into the tunnel—was gone!

Some one had broken the dam!

Into the empty plunge-hole, one after another tumbled the two big beavers. There was no time to be lost. They were losing their precious water, the water upon which the lives of their little ones so much depended! Their home was open now to all the world; it might mean the death of all of them. The four kittens terrified, realizing that something terrible was wrong but too young to know just what it might be, crept close together, whimpering, while their alarmed parents tore through what was left of the water, towards the dam.

They found a hole, nearly as big as a barrel, right at the deepest part of it, where it would quickly drain the lake to the very bottom. Madly the beavers began to work, pulling down sticks from anywhere, tearing out great armfuls of earth from the marshy shore, slashing off limbs from fallen trees with their razor-sharp teeth, rolling stones into the hole and shoving grass and brush in between them, digging up mud and pushing it before them into the break, where the suction of the now rapidly falling water held it plastered tight against the sticks and stones and brush. But the pond had been too small for so big a leak, and water was not coming from the tiny stream that fed it, nearly as fast as it was going out.

And now that the dam was almost repaired, the pond was empty!

Despair seized on the beavers (don't let any one ever tell you that animals cannot feel despair!) as they worked, but they never gave up until the very last load was in its place, and then, their task finished, they turned and plodded wearily and unhappily back towards their four little babies in the house, useless now as a protection—the house they had worked so hard to build, the babies that they loved so very much. Beavers are slow walkers, and what had once been a short, easy swim had now become a slow, awkward scramble through slippery mud and over rocks and tangled, fallen water plants and weeds. Precious minutes would pass before they would have staggered, and crawled, and dragged their way to that dark mound that now seemed so far away. Anything could catch them. If a bear or a wolf should pass and see them they would have no chance; the Beaver People were defenceless now, for they were never made to fight, only to work.

Hurry! Hurry! Gitchie Meegwon, run your fastest; your Little Brothers need you badly, need you now! Soon, any minute, he should be here——

Across the muddy bottom of the pond the two big beavers struggled slowly, painfully, and pitifully on their short and weary legs towards their unprotected home and babies, while, within the lodge, huddled together, their tiny hands clutched tightly in each other's woolly fur, four helpless little kitten beavers stared in terror at a sleek, black monster with a flat, evil head, that crept slowly through the entrance towards them, his teeth bared, hissing like a snake as he came. Negik* the Otter, the hungry, the cruel, and the sly, having broken the dam and

* Pronounced Nee-*gik* with the "g" hard as in "go."

so drained the pond, could now get what he had come for—
kitten beaver meat! Now was his time. His snaky body
blocked the plunge-hole; there seemed to be no escape. He
gathered his legs beneath him, ready to spring.

Just then Gitchie Meegwon, breathless, his shirt off, his gun
ready, burst through the reeds beside the dam, and leaping
from rock to rock, made for the beaver house.

IV

THE FIRST ADVENTURE

THE otter sprang. But in his eagerness he tried to seize the little beavers all at once, and they, quick as so many coiled springs, threw themselves sideways in the way that beavers have, and scattered before him as he came. Aiming at no particular one, he missed them all, nearly stunning himself against the wall of the lodge with the force of his leap. This confused him for a second, and the kittens rushed past him through the entrance, now no longer blocked by his body. The otter, roused to ferocious anger by his failure, and knowing very well that he could catch them one by one outside, was about to turn in pursuit, when the doorway was again darkened. That was all the warning he had. The next moment he was fighting for his life with the two big beavers. They had arrived only just in time; and they, usually so playful and good-natured, would fight to the death in defence of their young ones.

The otter was quicker on his feet and fiercer than they were, and could lock his jaws like a vise once he had bitten in, like a bull-dog; but a beaver's hide is tough, and the chisel-shaped teeth, that could hew down big trees and had never before been

27

used to do harm to any one, now slashed through skin and muscle, inches deep. They held on with their hands and drove their razor-edged cutting-teeth in deeper and deeper. The otter fought hard, for he was no coward, trying for his favourite hold on a beaver's nose and mouth, so as to prevent at least one of them from using its teeth. But he had all he could do to defend his own throat, at which the beavers were aiming. He twisted and turned like a great hairy lizard, lashing out right and left with his snaky head, hissing, snapping, and snarling. The beavers held on in deadly silence, while he dragged them from place to place, and they drove their teeth in again and again. For here was an enemy, the worst one of them all, who must be got rid of somehow—anyhow. Fighting fair with this evil beast was only a waste of time; the matter must be settled once and for all. Over and over they fought and wrestled and rolled, until they rolled right out through the plunge-hole, a squirming tangled mixture of legs, tails and glistening teeth, almost at the feet of Gitchie Meegwon, whose last flying jump from one rock to another had brought him close beside the beaver house. The sight of this new foe discouraged the otter completely, and with a violent effort he broke loose and in one leap was beyond the beavers' reach. Paying no attention to the Indian, they scrambled after the fleeing otter, but the slimy mud that held them back gave the otter just the kind of going that he needed, and he threw himself forward in the slippery ooze and slid twenty feet at one shot, took two or three jumps and another slide, and kept this up until he was at the dam, and over it, and away— forever.

Never again would he make war on the Beaver People!

Big Feather, standing on a nearby rock, saw his retreat. Once he aimed his rifle at the otter, but thinking he had punishment enough he let him go. Anyway, everything was all right now, and water was beginning to collect again. A good-sized pool had already formed in the basin of the pond, getting larger all the time and held there by the dam, which, as you remember, the beaver had repaired; and Big Feather was obliged to hurry back to shore before his rocks became covered again. However, he was still a little anxious, as he had seen the young ones rush out, but had not seen them go in. So he sat down on the shore, in a spot where he could be neither seen nor smelled, and watched the goings on. Soon he saw the mother beaver commencing to collect her little ones, one at a time. Two of them had come out of hiding, and as she came for them in turn, each would mount upon her broad, flat tail which trailed behind her like a short toboggan, and standing upright on it and holding onto his mother's fur with his hands to steady himself, would be dragged across the mud to the doorway. And the little fellows would look around them as they rode on this queer conveyance, taking in all the sights, no doubt feeling mighty pleased with themselves. I think Big Feather got as much fun out of it as they did; he saw two of them taken home this way and laughed to himself at the comical sight. And as he watched, he could not help feeling, somehow, that it was a great shame ever to kill such creatures, that worked so hard to protect their babies and their humble home, and seemed to have such real affection for each other—almost like killing little people, he thought. He had never before seen such things as had happened here today, and he began to realize why some of the older Indians called the beavers Little Talking Brothers, and Beaver People.

Although he had neither food nor blanket, he made up his mind to stay all night in case the otter should return, or another one come, for they often travel in pairs. But none did, and when Gitchie Meegwon left next morning he saw that the pond had filled up completely, and was running over as before; the secret doorway was again hidden and everything was in good order, and the same as it had ever been.

That is, nearly everything. What he did not know was, that two of the kittens, scared almost out of their wits, had scrambled on and on through one of the long passageways that beavers often dig for various purposes under the muskeg,* and coming to the end of it had found themselves near the dam. Trying to get as far away as they possibly could from that fierce monster, and hardly knowing or caring where they went, they had slipped over the dam unobserved. They had gone on down the now dry and empty stream-bed, hearing in their excited imagination the hissing breath of Negik close behind them. So real did this become to them, and so near did it seem to be at last that they scrambled hastily under a hollow in the bank— and not a moment too soon. For they were scarcely out of sight before the otter went hurrying by; they really had heard him. Fortunately, baby beavers, like the very young of many other animals, give out no scent, so that not even a fox, for all his

* A quaking bog, often partly afloat.

sharp, inquisitive nose, could ever have found them except by accident. So Negik never knew they were there, and kept on putting as much ground between himself and the beaver pond as he could.

Too terrified now to move lest their enemy should return, the two mites clung together in their shelter, afraid to go ahead, afraid to turn back. So they waited for their mother, who would be sure to look for them. But that lack of scent that had just now saved them from the otter, was to be their undoing. For their parents, searching frantically everywhere, could not trace them and never knew they had even left the pond; and in their excitement and fear the kittens had never noticed how short a distance they had really come. So, like two tiny lost children, they sat miserable and lonely in their little cave, listening for a deep, crooning voice that they loved, waiting, waiting for the big kind mother who had always comforted them in their small troubles and kept them warm with her brown, furry body and had combed and scrubbed them so carefully every day. Surely she, or their father, who had played so gently with them and taught them how to swim, and had always brought them sweet-grass for their beds and sprays of tender leaves for them to eat, would soon come for them! But now there were no sweet-grasses, no juicy tender leaflets, only hard rocks and gritty sand; and no father, no mother ever came for them. And so they crouched together all the long night, shivering, hungry, and afraid.

Once a slim, dark creature, the shape of a weasel but much larger, peered in at them, and they waited, still as two mice, scarcely daring to breathe, while he sniffed loudly at the opening where they were hidden, and then passed on. It had been a mink who, seeing two of them together, had feared to attack them. Later on they peered out cautiously from under the bank, but ducked back just in time to escape a great, grey shape that swooped down at them from above, an awful, ghostly creature with huge, staring yellow eyes, that missed them only by an inch or two and swooped up again, to sit on an overhanging branch. From the branch it stared and stared, and snapped its beak and gave loud, long screeches, and made a horrible chuckling sound.

Wap-aho,* the Laughing Owl of the woods, had spotted them and was waiting patiently for his chance. And every time they peered out from their hiding-place, the dreadful yellow eyes were there, staring down at them.

At daylight the owl was gone, and as the dam was full again and spilling over by now, the stream was running freely. And on its flow the beavers now set out to find their home. If they had only known how close it was! But the poor little heads were badly muddled now, and they were entirely lost. And, too small to swim against the current, they went the easiest way and floated with it, slipping down, down the stream, farther and farther away from their home, their parents, and the tiny sisters† they had romped and played with so happily all their short lives.

On they floated, weak and hungry for want of the leaves and

* Pronounced *Wop-a-ho*.
† Only the little males would have been so venturesome.

plants they did not know how to look for; yet they felt a little safer now that they were in the water once again—drifting along on this fruitless journey that could have only one ending. As the little stream began to reach the level of the Yellow Birch it flowed more slowly and became quieter and quieter, and they floated easily and smoothly upon its lazy waters. Once a deer, feeding in a shallows, looked up and saw them, watched them with his gentle eyes, his long ears pointed forward. Further on they met a hurrying muskrat, who gave them a sharp chitter of greeting and passed them by. Birds looked down on them and called to them from the tree tops, far above; and the sun was warm and pleasant, and the world was very beautiful as they floated sleepily, dreamily along—to nowhere. And so they would go on, dreamy with hunger and weakness until, as sick little beavers do, they would fall asleep at last and never wake.

Then, as they floated out onto the broad, calm waters of the Yellow Birch, Gitchie Meegwon saw them.

He had been back at his dinner place again, at the foot of the stream, and quietly launching his canoe he paddled softly over to them. They heard him, opened their eyes a little and saw him. Somehow they were not afraid, as he lifted them into the canoe by their tiny black tails. Perhaps they didn't care any more, or maybe the big watchful eye painted on the front of the canoe didn't look so sharp and fierce as it was intended to. Perhaps, too, they knew he wouldn't harm them; for animals, even very young ones, seem to know who is their friend.

He handled them very gently, for they were very small and pitiful as he held them cupped in the hollow of his two hands.

Their wee front paws were tucked up in feeble little fists,* as though to put up some kind of fight for their tiny lives; but the chubby heads were too heavy and drooped down, and their eyes were closed. Big Feather knew they must be dying, and was sorry for them. For he was a kindly man, as hunters so often are, when they stop to think.

He would try to save them. After all, he thought, he had made his living killing beavers for their fur, and it seemed only fair that in return he should do something for these two lost waifs that had drifted almost into his hands. On shore, he took from his provisions a can of milk, and making a thin mixture of some of it with water, poured a little in their mouths. And as he held the small woolly bodies gently in his big brown hands, he could feel how flat and empty their little stomachs were, and how feebly the little hearts were beating. And as he fed them they clutched tightly at his fingers with their tiny hands. And his heart softened more and more towards them as he fed them, though he hardly knew what he was going to do with them. He had little time to spare, as he had promised Sajo† and Shapian,‡ his children, that he would be back on a certain day, and he did not want to disappoint them. If he carried the kittens back to the pond they might never find their way across, and if he let them go here they would certainly starve, or else

---

* A beaver's attitude of defense. They are capable of striking quick, sharp blows, using the strong, heavy finger-nails, or with the hand balled into a fist. The latter device is used when it is desired to avoid inflicting injury with the nails, as among themselves. Note that the little beavers, even though at the last extremity, instinctively chose the gentler method. Such is their disposition.

† Pronounced *Say*-jo.   ‡ Pronounced *Shap*-ee-an.

the hawks, or an eagle, or even a hungry fish would get them. But he had far to go, and they would be a nuisance; after all they were only little animals—yet, they were in great trouble and needed help, and he felt that it would be wicked to abandon them; for some of the old-time Indians had very strict rules about such things.

Their mother had thought them very beautiful; but the Indian found them to be very homely indeed, with their big hind feet, short, round little bodies, and little pug noses, rather like Pukwajees,* or Indian fairies. In fact, they were so homely that really they were cute, he finally decided, just the thing for pets! Sajo, his little daughter, was nearly eleven years old, and was soon to have a birthday. They would make a fine present—the very thing! And when they became too big to have for pets, they could be brought back to their old home again. And just then, feeling the effects of the milk, they began to cry for more —those voices! They quite finished Gitchie Meegwon—how could a man desert two creatures that were able to cry so much like children, he asked himself, at the same time pouring some more milk down the hungry little throats.

And so he cut a large sheet of tough, leathery bark from a fine birch tree that stood close by among the pines, and with it made a strong, light box, or basket, with strips of cedar wood to hold it in its shape, made a close-fitting lid that fitted neatly down over the top of it, and punched it full of holes for air, and made a handle of braided cedar bark to carry it by. And inside it he put some bedding of grass and rushes, and green food-

* Pronounced *Puk*-wajees.

stuffs such as he knew that beavers loved. And when he lifted them in by their little flat tails (they made a first-class handle!), and they smelt the nice clean bed of sweet-grass, the very same as they had always had at home, and found the tender buds and leaves that they had been unable to find for themselves and that they had wanted so badly; and what with the kind, soothing voice of their new friend, and the way their little bellies were all filled up, and what with—oh, one thing and another, they suddenly felt very much better.

And they forgot the otter with his hissing, fishy breath, clean forgot the owl with his staring yellow eyes and fiercely snapping beak, who had laughed at them so grimly in the darkness. And they jabbered together with little bleats and squeals, as they had not done this long time past, and ate and ate until they could hold no more.

Big Feather, as he dipped and swung his paddle in his swift canoe, on his way back to his home and loved ones, was very pleased with the gift that he would bring his children (of course the boy, who was three years older than his sister, would have to share in the fun too, even though it was not his birthday); and he was glad because he had helped two suffering forest creatures. And speaking to the canoe, or his gun, or maybe to the little beavers, or perhaps just talking to himself, he said:

"Mino-ta-kiyah,* it is well! Kae-get mino-ta-kiyah, it is well indeed!"

And the two small adventurers must have found things to be

* Pronounced Mee-*no*-ta-*kiy*-ah.

& FEATHER CUT
SHEET OF BIRCH BARK,
MADE A BASKET FOR THE LITTLE BEAVERS"

G.O.

going very well with them, too, as they had become very quiet. Indeed, they were very comfortable on their nest; and they could hear, through the air holes in their birch-bark chamber, the song of the blackbirds and the thrushes, and the cheerful gurgling of the water all around; the drowsy humming of the insects and all the other pleasant woodsy sounds. Yet, even in this new-found happiness, they did not quite forget, never would quite forget, the kind father and mother, and the old home and small companions they had lost; and they were lonely for them all at once, so they whimpered a little and crept together and held each other tight. Then the loneliness would go away again, when they were close together, and the tired little heads nodded, and the little voices were quiet, and the round black eyes just would *not* stay open any more, and then the pleasant sounds outside faded quite away, and their troubles, at last, were altogether gone. And so they fell asleep.

And that is how two small, lost kitten beavers, so small that both of them could have sat together very comfortably in a pint-pot, went on their way to a new home and friends, and saw many strange and wonderful things that the wisest of beavers had never even heard about, and had adventures such as no beavers ever had before, I'm pretty sure.

It was indeed, as Big Feather had said, mino-ta-kiyah—really quite first class, in fact!

V

Sajo's Birthday

ONE day, almost a week later, Sajo and Shapian were busy preparing for their father's homecoming. Gitchie Meegwon's home was a short distance away from the Indian village of O-pee-pee-soway,* which means The Place of Talking Waters. The Indians had so named the village on account of a little low waterfall that was near by, where the bubbling and the murmuring of the water made a sound like that of low, dreamy voices, so that the people said that there were spirits in the falls.

The cabin in which they lived was built of pine logs, and stood not far from the lake shore, on a grassy knoll. The forest started right behind it, but all around the camp the ground had been cleared of underbrush and fallen timber, leaving only the finest trees, which formed a lovely glade through which there could be had a splendid view of the lake. This lake was a large one, and the farther shore showed only as a range of tumbled, forest-covered hills that seemed to be rolling forever on into the blue distance, like the waves of some great, dark ocean. A narrow footpath, or water-trail, led down the slope from the cabin to the landing, where stood a grove of tall and graceful poplar trees, in whose leafy shade Gitchie Meegwon and his young son and daughter spent many a happy Summer day beside the water, and often took their meals there.

* Pronounced O-pee-*pee*-soway.

38

The cabin was not large, but it made a handsome appearance from the outside, with its walls of red-brown logs and rows of green and yellow moss between them. Though it had only one room, it was even more pleasant to look at on the inside. The floor, of solid logs hewed flat and fitted tight together, had been scrubbed until it was as clean and bright as any floor you ever saw, and on the three bunks that stood in a row along one wall, rich-looking Hudson Bay blankets were neatly folded. Some of them were red, some were white, and others green, each with wide black stripes at either end, and they made the place look very gay and cheerful. The three windows, a single large pane of glass in each, were as spotless and shining as windows ought to be, as shiny as the inside of a rifle barrel, so Shapian put it; for that was his idea of something that was very clean indeed. That was the way he kept his own rifle, and today it had been oiled and rubbed, inside and out, till it fairly glittered in its corner, opposite the door where any one who entered could not help but see it. For this rifle, which had cost him four good mink skins at the Trading Post, was the proudest of all his possessions, which, I may tell you, were not very many.

Sajo had gathered the stems of bullrushes and dried them, and then cut them into short lengths and dyed them blue, and red, and yellow, and threaded them, like long, narrow wooden beads, on strings, and these hung down in rows beside the windows. She had arranged the different colours to make a kind of pattern, and they had quite an expensive look about them—rather like curtains she thought, as she glanced at them for about the hundredth time.

On the table, all the tin dishes and knives and forks had been arranged in their proper places, and in the center was a large loaf of Indian bread, or bannock, as it is called, freshly baked and still steaming hot, and stuck upright in the top of it was a very small spruce tree, no higher than your hand. It was really a tiny Christmas tree, and although it was not Christmas time, Sajo was nearly as happy as if it had been, and that was her way of showing how she felt about everything. The little iron stove that had been polished until it looked like a new one, had no oven and no legs, and was raised some distance from the floor on flat stones, which was a very convenient arrangement, as, to bake bread, all one had to do was to cook the dough for a while on top of the stove, and then put it underneath, between the warm stones, where it got finished off and nicely browned by the heat from the fire above. Otherwise the loaf would have had to be turned over in the pan when it was half baked, which would have made matters a little uncertain. And Sajo made good bread, I can tell you that, for I have eaten it many's the time.

Shapian had done his part too, as could be seen by the large pile of wood in a box behind the stove, and the rug of deerskin, newly stretched and dried, that lay in the center of the floor; while in a huge pot upon the stove, were cooking all the choicest portions of the meat—obtained with that so much-prized rifle in the corner. Shapian was a manly-looking boy, tall for his age, with the copper-coloured skin and dark eyes of his people, the Ojibways. He sat quietly waiting; his father had set this day for his return, and when he promised something he always kept his word, as nearly as the uncertainties of forest life would allow. But his sister, younger than he, her brown eyes aglow and her jet black hair, in two long braids, flying behind her, ran and hopped and skipped from place to place, tending to the cooking, placing around the table the rough wooden blocks they used for chairs, and putting the finishing touches to the wooden curtains.

Shapian had seated himself where he could get a good view out across the lake, through one of the windows, and was watching for the first sight of Big Feather's canoe—though he pretended not to be, and had picked a window on the far side of the room, through which he could keep an eye without appearing to do so. It would never do, he thought, to show how anxious he was. He was only fourteen, but he was feeling quite grown-up just now, as he had been the head of the household for well over a month. Sajo sang a little song as she worked, and was all aflutter with a many-coloured tartan dress, and on her dancing feet was a beautiful pair of beaded moccasins, worn only on special occasions. For this was to be a big day for her; not only was her so-loved father coming home, but it was her birthday. Poor Sajo, she did not often get a birthday gift since her mother had been laid to rest beneath the wild-flowers, but she still had two wooden dolls her father had made for her on two different birthdays. This year he had been away and would have had no time to make her anything. So the two dolls, Chilawee and Chikanee by name, had been brought out and were sitting on the edge of one of the bunks, not looking particularly cheerful, though they too were all dressed up in tartan plaid, as Sajo was, and their complexions, which had either soaked in or run off, had been renewed with a paint brush, and they each had a little head shawl round their wooden faces. They *did* look rather dumb, come to look at them; they had neither fingers nor noses nor mouths, but it is very likely that they didn't know the difference, and they would have to do for this time. At least, so Sajo thought, but we know differently, you and I, and she never guessed, as she went so happily about her tasks, the big surprise she was going to have.

Meanwhile Shapian sat very still and watched across the room, through his window, wishing that his sister would act a little more dignified and not be so wild and excited—still, two such big events as these coming both together on the same day, must be rather unsettling to a woman, he supposed. And then his own heart began to beat a good deal faster and he had all he could do to keep from rushing to the window; for out on the lake far, far away, he saw a tiny speck.

"Sister," he said, speaking slowly and distinctly, as was his fashion, "our father is coming."

"Where? Where?" cried Sajo, and without waiting for an answer she snatched up her head shawl and ran out through the door, looking eagerly in every direction. "Where, show me, quick!" Shapian pointed out over the water, to the speck.

"There," he said. "That little spot."

"Oh," said Sajo, and her voice fell a little; that spot could be anything. "Maybe it's a bear or a moose swimming," she suggested, hoping he would say it wasn't. But an answer came before he had time to speak.

Far off, faintly, they heard a sound, a faint, sharp crack—a rifle shot; and then, right away, another. They listened; there was a pause while you could count three, and then another shot.

"The signal! The signal!" cried Sajo, and Shapian replied quietly: "Yes, it is our father's signal," and then, quite forgetting himself, turned and rushed into the cabin with her, saying:

"Let us get ready quickly," and although the canoe was still some miles away and would not be in for at least an hour, there then commenced a great bustle as they went to work. They ran to the shelves for the jars of preserved blueberries and wild strawberries that Sajo put by every year though these were really the first she had ever done all by herself, but she had made a good job of them, and liked to feel that this had been going on for years and years. And they put on the big tea-pail to boil and stuck a long iron fork into the meat to see if it was cooked, and ran from table to stove and from stove to table and back again, and altogether acted a good deal like any other children would have done on such an occasion, whether they were rich or poor, or royalty, or just a couple of little Indians.

And when at last there came that long-looked-for moment when the yellow bark canoe, with its watchful eye and swaying tail, slid to a stop upon the sandy beach, everybody began to talk at once and Gitchie Meegwon stepped out on the shore and took their hands, or as many of them as he could hold in one of his, while he held the other, for some reason, behind him, and tried to answer all the questions at once, while his face, that could look so stern, was full of smiles and laughter as he cried:

"Children, children, let me speak, give me a chance to speak

—yes, I am safe, no, I didn't see any half-breeds, and yes, our hunting ground is not disturbed—or no, I should have said, and yes, I was lonesome, but not now, and—Happy Birthday to you my Sajo, Happy Birthday, my little daughter" and not till then did he bring out from behind his back the other hand. In it there was, just as we had guessed, the birch-bark basket, which he held by its braided handle up beyond their reach, and said:

"Gently, gently; see! I have brought you a gift for your birthday, Sajo," and gave it to her and told her to carry it with great care, while he turned to Shapian and added: "For you too, my son; there are two of them."

"Two of what, father?" asked the boy, looking after his sister, who had started away. "What is in the basket?"

But Big Feather said for him to wait and see. And they followed Sajo to the cabin as she went up the pathway at a funny little gliding run, supposed to be jolt-proof, so that while the small beaded moccasins twinkled in and out from under the tartan dress at a great rate, her body was held as stiff as possible from the knees up, so as not to jar the basket, which she held out in front of her as though it were a large and very delicate egg that would break into a thousand fragments at the slightest shock. Very carefully indeed she went, for out of this mysterious box there came the strangest sounds. A baby, she thought, no, two babies—though it seemed they must be very little ones to be in so small a space. Once inside, she set the basket very gently down upon the floor, and while Shapian (he had lost no time on the way either) held the sides, she took off the lid, and looking inside saw what you and I knew all the time were there

—two small, round woolly bodies and four little paws that reached for the edge of the box like tiny hands, and two pairs of bright black eyes, like shoe-buttons, that looked up at her so knowingly.

"Oooh!" she breathed, a kind of a gasp it was. "Oh! Oh!" And that's all she could say, and could think of nothing else to say and so said "Oh!" again; and at last:

"Teddy bears, live teddy bears," she cried, and then she turned the basket gently on its side and out they came; and she saw their tails and knew then what they were! Better than Teddy bears——

"Little beavers, it's little beavers," burst out Shapian, pale with excitement, his youthful dignity gone to the four winds, "real ones, alive!" while the tall Big Feather stood smiling down at the two delighted youngsters, very pleased indeed to see how well his present was received. Sajo sat beside them in wonder on the floor, her mouth still an "O," but no sound was coming out of it any more. And now she was too busy to draw her father's attention to the curtains she had been so proud of, although you may be sure his sharp eyes did not miss them; and the dinner was kept waiting and the famous gun, so clean and shiny, stood forgotten in its corner.

Gitchie Meegwon had looked after the kittens very carefully on the long journey, and had fed them well and they were round, and fat, and cuddly-looking, and Sajo thought they were the cutest things she had ever seen. And when they clambered onto her knees with little shaky whimpers, she bent down over them, and rubbed her face on their soft wool, that smelled so

sweet from their bed of scented grass and willow bark. Soon
Big Feather and Shapian went out to find fresh leaves and bedding for their small guests; but Sajo stayed behind. And while
these two were away, she picked the little beavers up and held
their dumpy little bodies, one at a time, in her two small hands,
where they fitted very comfortably, and whispered softly to
them—and, wonder of wonders, they answered her in little
childish voices, and held onto her fingers with their wee hands
(you could call them nothing else), and looked at her very
attentively out of their bright black eyes that seemed somehow
to look so very wise. And when she held them both together
in her arms they made funny little sounds, and pushed their
warm, damp noses tight against her neck, and blew and puffed,
as little babies do.

And she knew that she was going to love them very much.

And at that, Chilawee and Chikanee, the dolls, who had been
looking on rather gloomily up till now, seemed more disconsolate than ever, so to spare the poor creatures any further pain,
Sajo put them with their faces to the wall, back on the shelf
where they belonged.

And in that plain log cabin, far back in the forests of the
Northland, there were that day three very happy people: Gitchie
Meegwon, because his homecoming had been so glad a one;
Shapian, because his father had given him, too, a share in the
beavers and had praised his work besides; and Sajo, because of
the most wonderful birthday gift that she had ever had.

VI

Big Small and Little Small

THE kittens quickly took a liking to their new way of living, and although no human beings could ever quite take the place of their own parents, everything possible was done to make them feel at ease.

Shapian partitioned off the under part of his bunk with sheets of birch bark, leaving one end open; and this was their house, in which they at once made themselves very much at home. Gitchie Meegwon cut a hole in the floor and fitted down into it a wash-tub, for a pond—not much of a one perhaps, but it was as large as the plunge-hole had been, and they spent nearly half their time in it, and would lie on top of the water eating their twigs and leaves. Whenever they left the tub, they always squatted their plump little personalities upright beside it, and scrubbed their coats, first squeezing the hair in bunches with their little fists to get the water out. That done, the whole coat was carefully combed with a double claw that all beavers are provided with, one on each hind foot, for this purpose. All this took quite a while, and they were so businesslike and serious about it that Sajo would become as interested as they were, and would sometimes help them, rubbing their fur this way and that with the tips of her fingers, and then they would scrub away so much the harder.

It was their fashion, when drying themselves off this way, to raise one arm high above their heads, as far as it would go, and rub that side with the other hand, and being upright as they were, it looked as if they were about to dance the Highland Fling. They often sat up in this manner while eating the bark off small sticks, and as one or other of them held a stick crossways in his hands, rolling it round and round whilst the busy teeth whittled off the bark, he looked for all the world like some little old man playing on a flute. Sometimes they varied the show, and when the sticks were very slim they ate the whole business, putting one end in their mouths and pushing it on in with their hands, while the sharp front teeth, working very fast, chopped it into tiny pieces. The rattle of their cutting machinery sounded much the same as would a couple of sewing machines running a little wild, and as they held up their heads and shoved the sticks, to all appearances, slowly down their throats, they looked a good deal like a pair of sword swallowers who found a meal of swords very much to their taste.

They had to have milk for the first two weeks or so, and Sajo borrowed a bottle and a baby's nipple from a neighbour in the village, and fed them with it turn about. But while one would be getting his meal (both hands squeezed tight around the neck of the bottle!), the other would scramble around and make a loud outcry and a hubbub, and try to get hold of the bottle, and there would be a squabbling and a great confusion and the can of milk was sometimes upset and spilled all over; so that at last there had to be another bottle and nipple found, and Shapian fed one kitten while Sajo fed the other. Later on they were fed bannock and milk, which made things a little easier, as each had his own small dish which the children held for him. The beavers would pick up the mixture with one hand, shoving it into their mouths at a great rate; and I am afraid their table manners were not very good, as there was a good deal of rather loud smacking of lips, and hard breathing to be heard and they often talked with their mouths full. But they had one very good point, which not all of us have, and liked to put away their dishes when they were through, pushing them along the floor into a corner or under the stove; of course if there was a certain amount of milk-soaked bannock left in them, that was quite all right, so far as the beavers were concerned, and by the time the dishes had arrived at their destinations these remains had been well squashed and trampled on the line of march, and the floor would be nicely marked up with small, sticky beaver tracks, having sometimes to be partly scrubbed. Sajo always collected the little dishes and washed them up, as she did those of the "big people." Being fed separately, each of them came to look on one of the children as his special friend, and one of them would go to each when they were called. At first they had no names, and the children just called, "Undaas, undaas, Amik, Amik,* which means "Come here, come here, Beaver, Beaver." But a little later on Sajo remembered the day that the two wooden dolls had seemed to be looking on when the kittens first had come, and how these new arrivals had so quickly taken their place. Well, she

* Pronounced Am-*mick*.

thought, they may as well take their names too, and so she called the beavers Chilawee and Chikanee,* which means Big Small and Little Small. The larger one of the two was called Chilawee, or Big Small, and the not-so-large one was called Chikanee, or Little Small. And so they were all named; and the names suited them very well too, because after all, they *were* very small and they *did* look a lot like a pair of woolly toys that had come to life and stepped down off a shelf. It was not long before they got to know these names, and would always come out from the house under Shapian's bunk when called on; but the names sounded so much alike, that when one was called they both would come, and as they themselves were as much alike as two peas, the difference in size being not very great, it was often pretty hard to tell which was which. To make matters worse, they did not grow evenly; that is, one would grow a little faster than the other for a while, and then he would slacken down and the other would catch up, and get ahead of him. First one was bigger than the other, then the other was bigger than the one! And it would be discovered that Little Small had been Big Small for quite some time, whilst Big Small had been going around disguised as Little Small. No sooner would that be fixed up than they would change sizes again, and when they evened up, in the middle stages as it were, they could not by any means be told apart.

It was all very confusing, and Sajo had just about decided to give them one name between them and call them just "The Smalls," when Chilawee settled matters after a manner all his

* Pronounced *Chill*-a-wee and Chik-a-*nee*.

own. He had a habit of falling asleep in the warm cave under the stove, between the stones, and one day there was a great smell of burning hair, and no one could imagine where it came from. The stove was opened and examined, and swept off, and the stove-pipes were tapped and rapped, but the smell of burning hair was getting stronger all the time; until some one thought of looking *under* the stove, to discover Chilawee sleeping there unconcernedly while the hair on his back scorched to a crisp, and he was routed out of there with a large patch of his coat badly singed. This made a very good brand, something like those that cattle are marked with on a ranch, and it stayed there all Summer, making it very easy to tell who was who; and by calling one of them (the burnt one) *Chil*awee, and the other Chik*anee,* so as to be a little different, they got to know each his name, and everything was straightened out at last.

They were a great pair of little talkers, Chilawee and Chikanee, and were always jabbering together and sometimes made the strangest sounds. And whenever either of the children spoke to them, which was often, they nearly always answered in a chorus of little bleats and squeals. When there was any work going on, such as the carrying in of water, or wood, or the floor was being swept, or if the people laughed and talked more than usual, or there were any visitors, the two of them would come bouncing out to see what it was all about and try to join in, and they would cut all kinds of capers, and get pretty generally in the way. It had been found that if given any tidbits from the table, they always took them into their house to eat or store them. So when they, like bad children, got to be something of a nuisance to the visitors, they had to be bribed with bits of bannock to make them go back in again; but before long, out they would come for some more bannock, and take that in with them, and out again and so on. Very soon they got to know that visiting time was bannock time as well, and when mealtimes came around they knew all about that too, and would be right there, pulling and tugging at the people's clothes and crying out for bannock, and trying to climb up people's legs to get it. And of course they always got what they wanted, and would run off with it to their cabin under the bunk, shaking their heads and hopping along in great style.

They followed the children around continuously, trotting patiently along behind them; and their legs were so very short and they ran so low to the floor on them that their feet could hardly be seen, so that they looked like two little clockwork animals out of a toy-shop, that went on wheels and had been wound up and never *would* stop. Anything they found on the floor, such as moccasins, kindling wood, and so forth, they dragged from place to place, and later, when they got bigger and stronger, they even stole sticks of firewood from the wood-box and took them away to their private chamber, where they sliced them up into shavings with their keen-edged teeth and made their beds with them; and nice, clean-looking beds they were too. Any small articles of clothing that might happen to fall to the floor, if not picked up at once, quickly disappeared into the beaver house. The broom would be pulled down and hauled around, and this broom and the firewood seemed to be their favourite playthings; greatly, I suspect, on account of the noise they could make with them, which they seemed very much to enjoy.

But their greatest amusement was wrestling. Standing up on their hind legs they would put their short arms around each other as far as they would go, and with their heads on each other's shoulders, they would try to put each other down. Now this was hard to do, as the wide tails and the big, webbed hind feet made a very solid support, and they would strain, and push, and grunt, and blow until one of them, feeling himself slipping, would begin to back up in order to keep his balance, with the other coming along pushing all he could. Sometimes the loser would recover sufficiently to begin pushing the other way and then the walk would commence to go in the opposite direction; and so, back and forth, round and round, for minutes at a time, they would carry on this strange game of theirs, which looked as much like two people waltzing as it did anything else. All the while it was going on there would be, between the grunts and gasps, loud squeals and cries from whoever was getting pushed, and much stamping of feet and flopping of tails, trying to hold their owners up, until one of them, on the backward march, would allow his tail to double under him, and fall on his back, when they would immediately quit and scamper around like two madcaps. It was all done in the greatest good humour, and the two children never grew tired of watching them.

Between this uproarious exhibition, and the flute-playing, and the sword-swallowing, and the begging, the trundling around of wood and all the other racket and commotion that, on some days, only ceased when they went to sleep, the beavers were about as busy, and noisy, and amusing a pair of little people as you could wish to live with.

But they were not always so lively. There came times when they were very quiet, when they would sit solemnly down together with their hands held tight to their chests and their tails before them, watching whatever was going on, still as two mice, looking, listening without a word, as though they were trying to make out what everything was all about. And sometimes, as they squatted there one beside the other, like two chocolate-coloured kewpies or little mannikins, Sajo would kneel in front of them and tell them a story, marking time to the words with her finger before their noses, as though she were conducting an orchestra. And they would sit there and listen, and watch her finger very closely, and soon they would commence to shake their heads up and down and from side to side, as beavers always do when they are pleased, and at last they would shake their whole bodies and their heads so hard that they would topple over and roll on the floor, exactly as if they had understood every word and just couldn't help laughing themselves to pieces over the story.* Shapian would stand by taking it all in, and finding it rather ridiculous; but at the same time he wished, very privately of course, that he was not quite such a man, so he could join in this story-telling business himself. There were

* This is actual fact, as are all the animal actions described in the story. Young beavers, raised by hand, will often respond in this manner to the advances of a person they know well. Wild beavers communicate their emotions to one another in this and other very striking ways.

"...EY WOULD SIT AND LISTEN AS THOUGH THEY UNDERSTOOD EVERY WORD ... AND THEN ROLL ON THE FLOOR AS IF THEY COULDN'T KEEP FROM LAUGHING"

times when this thing of being grown up rather interfered with
the fun!

Sometimes the little fellows were lonely and would whimper
together with small voices in their dark little chamber, and
Sajo, who had never forgotten her own mother and knew why
they were lonesome, would take them in her arms and croon
softly to them, and try to comfort them. And they would
snuggle up close to her, holding tight to each other's fur all the
while as though afraid to lose one another, and would bury
their wee noses in the warm, soft spot in her neck where they
so loved to be; and after a while the whimpering would cease
and they would perhaps forget, for this time, and they would
give big, long sighs and little moans of happiness, and fall
asleep. For after all, with all their mischief and their shouting
and their fun, they were just two small lost waifs, and they gave
to these two human children, in their own humble way, the
same love they had given to the father and the mother they had
lost, and whom they never would forget.

And especially Chikanee loved Sajo. Chikanee was not as
strong as Chilawee, was quieter and more gentle. Chilawee had
a rather jolly way about him and was more of a roisterer, one
of those "all for fun and fun for all" kind of lads to whom life
is just one big joke; but Chikanee often had lonesome spells
by himself, in corners, and had to be picked up and petted and
made much of. Often he came out in the night and cried beside
Sajo's bed to be taken up and allowed to sleep there beside her
—while Chilawee lay on his back in the hut, snoring away like
a good fellow. When Chikanee was in some small trouble,

such as bumping his nose on the stove, or getting the worst of a wrestling match, he came to Sajo for comfort, and Sajo, always ready to sympathize with him because he was the weaker of the two, would kneel down beside him on the floor; and then Chikanee would climb onto her lap and lie there, happy and contented. Chilawee, when his badness was all done for the day, and he was feeling perhaps a little left out of things, would come over to get *his* share of the petting, squeezing in tight beside Chikanee, where he would settle down after giving a few deep sighs, vastly pleased, no doubt, with his day's work. And Sajo, not wishing to disturb them, would stay there until they were ready to go.

It was very easy to tell them apart by now, as they had become quite different in their ways. Chilawee was stronger, bolder, and more adventurous than his chum, a kind of comical fellow who seemed to enjoy bumping his head on the table legs, or dropping things on his toes, or falling into the wood-box. He was as inquisitive as a parrot and wanted to be into everything, which he generally was, if he could reach it. Once he climbed up onto the edge of a pail of water that some one had left on the floor for a moment, and perhaps mistaking it for a plunge-hole, dived right into it. The pail, of course, upset with a bang, splashing the water in all directions. Chilawee was most surprised; and so was everybody else. But in spite of all this wilful behaviour, he was just as affectionate as Chikanee, and dogged Shapian's footsteps (when not otherwise engaged!) nearly as much as the other one did Sajo's. And he could not bear to be away from Chikanee very long. Everywhere they went they were together, trotting along one behind the other, or side by side, and if they should become parted on their wanderings in the camp, they would start out to look for each other, and call to one another. When they met they would sit quite still for a little time, with their heads together, holding each other by the fur—though this wistful mood soon passed off, and it was not long before it all ended up in one of those queer wrestling matches, which seemed to be their way of celebrating.

And Sajo often thought how cruel it would be ever to part them.

VII

The Trader

THERE came a time when Big Feather said that the kittens should be allowed their freedom. They were now quite a size, and very active and strong, and the children were a little afraid that they would wander off and be forever lost. But their father told them how little beavers will not leave their home, if kindly treated, but would always return to the cabin as if it were a beaver house. He said they got lonely very quickly and would only stay away an hour or two.

So, one great, glorious, and very exciting day, the barricade that had been kept across the bottom of the doorway was taken away, and out they went. Not all at once though, as they did a lot of peeping and spying around corners, and sniffed and listened to a whole host of smells and sounds that were not really there at all. They made two or three attempts before they finally ventured down to the lake, with Sajo and Shapian on either side for a bodyguard. They started off at a very slow and careful walk, sitting up every so often to look around for wolves and bears; of course there weren't any, but it was lots of fun pretending. And as they came closer to the lake the walk became faster and broke into a trot, which soon became a gallop and into the water they rushed—and then dashed out again, hardly knowing what to make of so large a wash-tub as this. However, they soon went in again, and before very long were swimming, and diving, and screeching, and splashing their tails and having a glorious time "Just like real beavers," said Sajo.

It wasn't long before they commenced to chew down small poplar saplings. These they cut into short lengths, and peeled the bark off them in great enjoyment, while they sat amongst the tall grass and the rushes at the water's edge. They played and wrestled, and ran up and down the shore, and romped with their young human friends, and tore in and out of the water in a great state of mind. They stuck their inquisitive noses into every opening they saw, and found in the bank an empty muskrat hole. As they were just about the same size as the late owner of the hole, this suited them exactly, and they started to dig. The opening was under water, and as they worked away there the mud began to come out in thick clouds, so that nothing in the water could be seen. And for a long time the beavers disappeared until, becoming alarmed, Shapian waded into the water and pushed his arm inside the hole and felt around. The beavers were not there! "Sajo" he called excitedly, "they are gone!" And the two of them commenced hurriedly to search among the reeds and brush along the shore, when they heard behind them a most forlorn wailing and cry-ing, and there, following them, running as fast as their stumpy little legs would carry them, came Chilawee and Chikanee, scared half to death for fear that they were being left behind. They had left their work, and, swimming away under the muddy water, they had slipped away, and had landed further down the shore without being seen.

And now they were tired. So, sitting down like two little furry elves, they scrubbed, and rubbed, and combed their coats, and when that was done and they were quite dry, they turned and walked slowly and solemnly, side by side, up the pathway to the house. And there, with a big chunk of bannock apiece, they slipped quietly away into their birch-bark bedroom and ate their lunch; and then squeezing as tightly together as they could get on their nice, dry bed of shavings, fell fast asleep. And that was the end of their first, great day of freedom.

At last they were, as Sajo had said, Real Beavers.

Every day after that, as soon as the door was opened, they trotted down to the lake and had their daily swim. They spent hours at a time digging out the burrow they had found, and when it was far enough back to be safe, as they considered (you would have thought from the way they sometimes watched and snooped around, that the country was full of dragons), it was turned upwards and made to come out on top of the ground, and so became a plunge-hole, and over it, to the intense delight of Sajo and Shapian, they built a funny little beaver house! So now they had a real lodge, with a small chamber in it and an under-water entrance, a tunnel and a plunge-hole, all complete. The lodge was a little shaky about the walls, and was not very well plastered, but it was really quite a serviceable piece of work, considering.

Then they collected a quantity of saplings, and poplar and willow shoots, and made a tiny feed raft with them in front

"BUILT THEMSELVES A CRAZY LITTLE BEAVER HOUSE"

of their water-doorway, as grown-up beavers do, although it was ever so much smaller. Of course, all this feed would become sour in the water long before it could be used, and the Summer was no time for feed rafts anyway, and the wobbly house could never keep out the rain; but little they cared! They had a warm bed of their own up in the cabin, and there was always plenty of bannock, and, on certain occasions, even a taste or two of preserves, and each had his own little dish to eat it out of, so that counting everything, they owned a considerable amount of property for the size of them and were really quite well-to-do. So they didn't need either the crazy-looking lodge or the feed raft, but it was great fun fixing things up and cutting little trees, and digging, and playing with mud (mud houses must be so much more interesting to make than mud pies!) and doing all those things that beavers like so much to do, and cannot live contentedly without.

Sajo and Shapian, who spent nearly all their time down there, were having just as good a time looking on, often helped as well, and any building materials such as sticks, brush, earth, or the odd stone that they brought down, was immediately pounced on by the two little beavers and carried away. And sometimes these young scallawags would come ashore covered with mud from head to foot, and try to climb all over their friends, and then there would be a regular scramble, and a great deal of laughter.

Shapian built a play-house by the water-side, and they were often all in there together, while they rested in the shade of it, and this was Chikanee's favourite spot, and he often went there to look for Sajo, and would always come there when she called him. But Chilawee, the adventurer, who was more of a rover, and something of a pirate I'm inclined to think, could not stay still anywhere very long, would soon ramble away, and was continually getting lost. Of course *he* knew he wasn't lost, but the others thought he was, which amounted to the same thing so far as they were concerned; and then of course there would be a hunt. And he would turn up in the most unexpected places, and would be found in the play-house when it was supposed to be empty, or in the cabin when he was supposed to be in the play-house, or hidden away in the beaver wigwam, or under the canoe, where he would be asleep as likely as not. And when found, he would sit upright with his tail up in front of him, and would teeter-totter and wiggle his body and shake his head, as if he were either dancing or laughing at the trick he had played on the rest of them. If there was a sudden and unreasonable commotion anywhere, it was nearly always safe to say that this scapegrace was at the bottom of it, and when there was any shouting, or squealing, or any kind of an uproar going on, Chilawee was always at his best—or his worst, whichever way you happened to look at it, and his voice could be heard calling from all kinds of places at all kinds of times.

Nor was Chikanee quite the saint you may begin to think he was; he had as much fun as any of them. But there were times when he would break off quite suddenly, as though some thought had come into his little head, perhaps some dim memory of his home-pond that was so far away among the Hills of the Whispering Leaves. And then, if Sajo were not there to comfort him, he would waddle on his squat little legs, up to the play-house to look for her. If he found her there, he would sit beside her and do his careful toilet; and after he was all tidied up, he would nestle close to this so well-loved companion, and with his head on her knee, try to talk to her in his queer beaver language and tell her what the trouble was; or else lie there with his eyes half closed and dreamy, making small sounds of happiness, or perhaps of lonesomeness, or love—we cannot know. Very, very good friends indeed were these two, and where one was, there would be the other, before very long.

And what with all the lively antics, and the skylarking, and the work (not too much of it of course) and all the play, it would be hard for me to tell you just who were the happiest among these youngsters of the Wild, those with four legs, or those with two. But this I *do* know, that they were a very merry crew, in those happy, happy days at O-pee-pee-soway, The Place of Talking Waters.

.   .   .   .

The tidbits of bannock had been getting smaller and smaller. Big Feather had been away some days now for more provisions and had not yet returned, and now there was hardly any flour. Nobody, children or beavers, had very much to eat, until one day the four playfellows arrived back at the cabin to find Gitchie Meegwon there.

He looked very grave and troubled about something. But the provisions were there; a bag of flour and some other goods lay on the floor, and beside them stood a white man, a stranger.

This man had with him a large box. Big Feather spoke kindly to his children, but without smiling as he generally did, and they wondered why. The white man, too, stood there without speaking. Somehow things didn't look right. Even the little beavers seemed to feel that there was something amiss, for animals are often quick to feel such things, and they too, stood there quietly, watching.

Shapian, who had been to Mission school and understood English fairly well, heard his father say to the man:

"There they are; which one are you going to take?"

What was that? What could he mean? With a sudden sick feeling Shapian looked at his sister; but of course she had not understood.

"Wait till I have a look at them," said the stranger, answering Big Feather's question: "Let them move around a bit." He was a stout, red-faced man with hard blue eyes—like glass, or ice, thought Shapian. But Big Feather's eyes were sad, as he looked at his boy and girl. He asked the white man to wait a moment while he spoke to his children.

"Sajo, Shapian; my daughter, my son," he said in Indian, "I have something to tell you."

Sajo knew then that some trouble had come to them. She came close to Shapian, and looked timidly at the stranger— why! oh why, was he looking so hard at the beavers!

"Children," continued their father. "This is the new trader from the fur-post at Rabbit Portage; the old one, our good friend, has gone. A new Company has taken over the post, and they ask me to pay my debt. It is a big debt, and cannot be paid until we make our hunt, next Winter. The other Company always dealt that way with the Indians, but the new Company say they cannot wait. We now have no provision, as you know, and this Company will give me nothing until the debt is paid. So I must go on a long journey for them, with the other men of the village, moving supplies to the new post at Meadow Lake, which is far from here. My work will pay the debt, and more, but I will receive no money until I return. In the meantime you, my children, must live. I cannot see you go hungry. This trader will give us these provisions"—here he pointed at the bags and parcels lying on the floor—"and in exchange he wants—he wants one of the beavers." He stopped, and no one so much as moved, not even the beavers, and he continued, "Live beavers are very valuable, and whichever one he takes will not be killed. But my heart is heavy for you, my children, and"—he looked at Chilawee and Chikanee —"and for the little beaver that must go."

Shapian stood very still and straight, his black eyes looking hard at the trader, while Sajo, hardly believing, whispered, "It isn't true. Oh, it isn't true!"

But Shapian never spoke, only put his arm around his sister's shoulder and stared hard at this man, this stranger who had come to spoil their happiness. He thought of his loaded gun, so close behind him in the corner; but his father must be obeyed, and he never moved. And he looked so fiercely at the trader that, although Shapian was only a fourteen-year-old boy, the man began to feel a little uneasy; so he opened his box, and reaching out for one of the beavers, picked the little fellow up, put him in it, and shut the lid. He nodded to Gitchie Meegwon:

"Well, I'll be seeing you down at the post in a couple of days," he said, and walked out with the box under his arm, shutting the door behind him.

Then Sajo, without a sound, fell to her knees beside her brother and buried her face in his sleeve.

The trader had chosen Chikanee.

And Chilawee, not knowing what to think, suddenly afraid, went into his little cabin, alone.

VIII

Sajo Hears the Talking Waters

THE next day Big Feather started away for the fur-post, on his way to work out his debt to the Company. With him were seventeen other men from the village, in three big bark canoes. At Rabbit Portage they would load up the canoes with supplies for Meadow Lake, or Muskodasing,* another of the Company's posts, far to the North. The brigade, as such canoe caravans are called, would be gone a month or more. And Sajo, Shapian, and Chilawee were left alone at O-pee-pee-soway.

When the trader had so sharply shut the door between her and the one thing, next to her father and her brother, that she loved most in all the world, it had seemed to Sajo as if the door had closed on her heart as well, and that it too had gone out with Chikanee, in the box.

After this, a big change had come over all three of them. The happy circle had been broken up. There were no more merry parties in the play-house, no more fun or laughter on the lake shore. Chilawee cut no capers any more, and his voice, that used to be heard at all times and everywhere, was still. He never did his funny, jolly dance and never played, but wandered miserably up and down the water-trail all the day long, searching for Chikanee. He couldn't seem to get it into

* Pronounced Mus-ko-*day*-sing.

his little head that his playmate was gone. He would start out fresh and hopeful every morning, at a little trot, feeling sure that he would find him somewhere, looking in every corner of the play-house, and running from one to another of the trampled places in the grass and reeds, where they had so often sat together and combed themselves, and wrestled, and basked in the sunlight. He swam up and down along the shore, searching at all their old landing places, and dived in and out of the shaky little lodge that it had been such fun to build.

So he hunted all day, until at last he would give up, and his eager, shuffling trot would become a slow and weary walk, and he plodded on his tired little legs, up the pathway to the camp and lay, without a sound, in his empty, silent hut—no longer a rollicking pirate, no more a mischievous scapegrace, but just a lonely, sorrowful little beaver. He was not Big Small any more, just Small, because now he was all the Small there was. The two children followed him on his rounds, and pretended they were looking too, though they know his search was useless; for they could not bear to see him hunting around all by himself, like an unhappy little ghost. And when he ate from his dish, they both sat down beside him and held it for him; sometimes there would be one or two big tears fall into the bread and milk when Sajo thought of Chikanee, who should have been there too—poor Chikanee, poor Little Small who had been so soft and gentle and who had often been so lonesome, now away somewhere in the great city, where there was no more romping, no more bannock, no more fun.

Somehow it seemed that he couldn't be really gone. You

more than half expected to find the squat little figure sitting somewhere in the play-house, or see a short-legged dumpy little body come bouncing out beside Chilawee from the birch-bark cabin for his daily feast of bannock, and almost any minute you were ready to declare that you had heard his voice down at the landing. Even his little tracks, much smaller than Chilawee's, ugly, intoed, and pathetic, were still there in the mud beside the water. Sajo would go very often to look at them, and when no one was near she knelt down and touched them gently with her fingers and whispered to them; until at last they were washed away and disappeared. Over the very last one that was left she laid a sheet of birch bark, and every day made a visit to it alone; but even it gradually dried out and faded to dust, and was soon quite gone.

And then there was nothing left of him at all.

Though Chilawee's voice was seldom heard these days, yet sometimes in the night he awoke and, whimpering in utter loneliness, groped in the darkness for another small, round body that he could never find. And Sajo would hear him and awaken, and would creep into his chamber with him, and lie beside him on his little bed of shavings and hold him close to her, sobbing, until they both would fall asleep again.

Shapian sat for hours looking out over the lake, staring across at the far-away, forever marching hills, saying nothing, his heart aching for his sister, who never sang or laughed around the cabin any more. And a lump would come in his throat—and then he would look around very fiercely; for no one must ever know how hard it was to keep back the tears.

How he hated those bags and parcels the trader had exchanged for Chikanee! The bannock nearly choked him when he ate it. If only he had thought to offer the trader his gun; four mink skins it had cost, and surely it was worth as much as one small, very small kitten beaver!

Although they had shared their pets, and Chilawee was really his, Shapian gave him up entirely to his sister. And she would sometimes take the little beaver, and carry him quite a distance up a creek that came tumbling down from out the hills behind the village, to where there was a low waterfall. Beside the fall there was a great, whispering pine tree and here, beneath the tree, she would sit and try to think of some way to get Chikanee back, while Chilawee swam, and dived, and even played a little by himself, in the quiet, deep pool below. He seemed happier there, Sajo thought, because the pool was small, and did not seem so wide and empty as did the lake, with its miles and miles of distance all around and only one small beaver there to fill it up.

And while her small companion swam around, or peeled his willow sticks, and sometimes sat upon her lap and combed himself, Sajo would listen to the voices in the falls. For, if you wait very patiently beside rapids or a waterfall you seem to hear, after a time, the sound of low murmuring voices, voices that come and go, now louder, now softer, sometimes seeming quite distinct, then fading away to be lost again in the muttering of the water. All the Indians have heard these sounds, and white people who have listened say they too can hear them, soft and singing in the brook. The Indians say that these are the voices of people from the Spirit Land, come back to speak to those they love. And here Sajo would sit until the voices came, and try to make out what they were saying. She was sure that some day she would be able to understand them, which was indeed likely, because Indian language so much resembles the sound of running water, the sighing of the wind, and the whispering of the trees. And Chilawee often sat beside her very quietly, as if he were listening, and perhaps he heard them too, better even than Sajo did, for a beaver's ears are much sharper than a person's.

This was the spot that the Indians called O-pee-pee-soway, The Place of Talking Waters, for which the village and the country round about were named. It had been Sajo's favourite place ever since she had been a very little girl, whenever she was lonesome, or wanted to think, or make up her mind about something. Often she would lie in the shade of the great pine, looking up into the dark, shadowy caverns between the giant branches; and when the sunbeams glanced through them and shone into those darksome caves, it looked very beautiful up in there, like some far-off, undiscovered country where there were fairies and other strange beings, and she sometimes wondered if that was where the spirits lived who spoke to people from the Talking Water. And as she lay gazing up into the gently swaying pine-top, listening to the stream, she used to feel somehow that her mother was near, speaking to her; and this made her very happy.

One day, as she sat there with Chilawee in her lap, listening to the drowsy murmur of the little fall, the sounds seemed to become very clear and plain, and she leaned back against the tree and shut her eyes, so as to hear them better. And after a while the sound of the water became less and less, and soon died quite away; and she thought that she could hear in place of it, some one speaking very softly, very plainly there beside her. Soon she began to make out the words, and the words were in the Indian language, that sounds so much like running water: "Sajo, Sajo, mah-jahn, mah-jahn. Sajo, Sajo, 'den-na jah-dahn," repeated over and over again, like a rhyme of poetry, or a song:

> Sájo, Sájo,
> Máh-jahn, máh-jahn.
> Sájo, Sájo,
> 'Den-na jah-dahn.*

> Sajo, Sajo,
> You must go.
> To the city
> You must go.

On and on the voice seemed to chant these words, now louder, now softer, the sound coming and going as the murmur of the water in the falls had done. And it became so plain at last, that she seemed even to recognize the voice, a voice she had not heard for so long, her mother's voice. And she cried:

"O my mother, here is Sajo; O my mother, tell me more. I will listen to the words you tell me." And she reached out

* The J's are all pronounced soft, as in "zh" or "zsh" except in the name Sajo, where the J is hard as in "John." Accent on all first syllables.

towards the sound and touched something soft and warm, and she opened her eyes rather suddenly to find her hand on the warm, damp nose of Chilawee, who was sitting up on her lap, pulling at her head shawl. She knew then that she had, for a moment, been asleep; and the words were lost again in the singing of the water, and the falls murmured on and on as they had always done.

Then Sajo jumped to her feet and took Chilawee up, and said to him:

"Chilawee, Chilawee, we are going to get Chikanee; we must go to the City for Chikanee. My mother has told me. I *know*."

So carrying the little beaver in her arms she started to run home, and as she ran she said to herself, yes, it was the voice of my mother. The Great Spirit let her come to the waterfall and speak to me; and she told me to go to the City—just wait till I tell Shapian!

And who can say that the Great Spirit of the Wild Lands, who watches over all the Little People, did *not* guide the waters while she slept, so they should seem to speak?

Meanwhile Chilawee got all shaken up with the running and didn't like it a bit, and he struggled to get down and began to cry out at the top of his voice, as he had not done for many a long day. Sajo thought, "He's got his voice back again, as before Chikanee went away, and that means my dream will come true. I *know* it will"; and she ran so much the harder. And between the running of one, and the calling out of the other, both of them were pretty well out of breath when they arrived at the cabin. And Shapian, seeing them in this state, came quickly out of the door and asked what the matter was; and Sajo told him of her dream, and how they must certainly go to the City.

But Shapian was not so ready to agree; he hadn't yet had time to think it over, and besides he hadn't had any dream. So he said:

"This is foolish, my sister; the City is far, we don't know the way, we have no money, and without money we can get neither bed nor food there; besides we would have to take Chilawee; and what would our father say?"

This all sounded very discouraging, but Sajo was not to be so easily turned aside, once she had made up her mind, and she answered:

"Our father is as sorry as we are, and would be glad if we found Chikanee again; for none of us have been happy since he was taken away."

But she said nothing about how she thought they were going to get to the City, or about what they would do if they did get there. For she believed very firmly in the message she had heard, and was quite positive that something wonderful was bound to come of it.* And Shapian looked at his sister and saw how her eyes were shining with hope, and how suddenly joyful she had become. To do as she asked would be hard, he knew, the hardest thing he had ever tried; but to refuse, without even

---

* It is customary among the more primitive Indians to decide on a course of action in accordance with a particularly vivid dream.

SAJO RAN HOME WITH CHILAWEE IN HER ARMS.

trying, and then to see her more broken-hearted than ever, would be harder yet. And his father had said, before he left, for him to do all he could to make her happy once again. So there was only one thing to be done.

"Yes," he said, "we will go." And he stood up very straight, in the way he had, and looked very firm and manly. "Yes. I will take you to the City. Tomorrow."

But for all he looked so stern and proud, Shapian had not the faintest idea of how he was going to set about it, nor did he ever guess what a desperate adventure this would turn out to be.

IX

THE RED ENEMY

LATE the same night, everything was in readiness for the journey. It would take Sajo and Shapian nearly a week to get to the trading post at Rabbit Portage, the first step of their long journey to the city; and they had no idea what lay beyond the post. So they took plenty of everything that was needed for a long trip. Sajo had made several large bannocks, and filled different-sized canvas bags with flour, tea, and salt, and she made up a parcel of dried deer meat and set aside a small pail of lard, and put matches in a tight-topped can where they would remain dry; while Shapian rolled up a tent and blankets, fixed up a fish-line, sharpened his belt-axe and his hunting knife, whittled a thin edge on the blades of the paddles, and boxed up whatever pots and dishes and other small items of cookery they would have need of.

The sun had not yet arisen on the following morning, when breakfast was over and the full outfit was loaded in the canoe, along with Shapian's rifle; for much as he prized this gun, he intended to sell it if he could, hoping that it would bring at least enough to pay their way to the city. What was to happen after that he didn't dare even to think about. Chilawee went in the same birch-bark basket in which he and Chikanee had first come to O-pee-pee-soway, and in the cookery-box Sajo had put *both* the little beaver dishes, as this helped her to feel more

76

certain that they were going to bring back Chikanee and Chilawee together.

"We will need them both," she said aloud, "for," and here
her voice dropped a little, "we *are* going to get him, I think,"
and then louder, as she nodded her head and pursed her lips, "I
just *know* we are." And to make her belief the stronger she
added, "My mother said so. In the sound of Mudway-oshkay.*
I heard her, in the sounding of the water she has told me!"

You see her dream seemed so very real, and meant so much
to her.

The village was some distance away from their cabin, and
they had told no one about their plans, for fear the older people
might try to stop them. The old Chief especially might forbid
them. So they slipped away into the mists of early morning
without any one being the wiser. And as they floated out from
the landing, Sajo shook her paddle above her head, as she had
seen the men do when they started on a journey, shouting the
name of the place they were bound for; and so she held her
paddle up and cried out "Chik-a-*nee!* Chik-a-*nee!*" You could
hardly call Chikanee a place but, she thought, wherever he is,
that's where we are going. But Shapian did not wave his paddle,
nor did he shout; for he was not so sure where they would end
up.

And so they left the Place of Talking Waters, and started out
on what was to be, for all three of them, their Great Adventure.

The canoe was the one with the eye and the tail, the same

* Pronounced Muh-*dway-oshe*-kay.

canoe in which we first saw Gitchie Meegwon on the River of Yellow Birches, and in it they paddled swiftly all that day, the great eye staring eagerly ahead and the fox's tail fluttering gaily out behind, as the canoe fairly leaped forward at every stroke of the paddles. They stopped occasionally in order to put Chilawee over the side to have a drink, and to swim around for a minute or two so as to get cooled off, for the weather was very hot. That night they put up their tent in the woods along the shore, and spent the night there. The next morning at daybreak they were away again, and paddled steadily till dark, stopping only to eat and to exercise their furry chum. Each morning they were on their way before the sun rose, and every evening they made camp in some sheltered spot beside the water, where Chilawee swam around all night, always returning to the tent at daylight to fall asleep in his basket, where he remained quietly all day. Both children worked on the portages, of which there were a number, each carrying his share of the load. There were two trips apiece, including the canoe, which Shapian carried alone. Neither of them found this to be particularly hard work; in fact, they thought nothing at all about it one way or the other, for that kind of a journey was nothing new to either of them.

And so, day after day they forged ahead, onward, onward, ever onward; and two small backs bent and swayed like clockwork and two paddles swished and dipped all the long day, as regularly and evenly as the step of marching soldiers, while the burning sun rose on one side of them, passed overhead, and sank again like a great red ball behind the dark wall of the forest.

Day after day the faithful bark canoe carried them staunchly and steadily forward, outward bound on the long search for the absent Chikanee.

And in all that great wilderness they were just a little moving speck that crawled across the silver surface of wide, boundless lakes, alone on the face of all the world; but it was a speck that held two young hearts that were full of courage and one, at least, that was high with hope—and another whose owner was full of bannock, and who lay snoring contentedly, even if not too happily, in his basket.

One morning they awoke to find a faint smell of wood-smoke in the air, a smell of burning moss and scorching brush and leaves, and they knew that somewhere, seemingly far away, there was a forest fire. But it was closer than they had at first supposed, for as soon as they were well out on the lake and were able to look about them, they could see an immense pillar of smoke billowing up from behind the distant hills; and they did not paddle very far before they found that their route would bring them more and more in its direction. The lake was getting very narrow, and farther on it ended and became a river, across which the fire could easily jump. Shapian determined to get through this narrow place as quickly as possible, to a large lake that lay beyond, where they would be safe. So they hurried on, and as they went the smoke spread higher and wider, so that it was no longer a pillar, but a white wall that seemed to reach the sky, and rolled outwards and down in all directions, becoming thicker and thicker until the sun was hidden, and the air became heavy and stifling, and very still. The whole country to the Eastward seemed to be on fire, and although the blaze itself was hidden by the hills, even at that distance there could be heard a low moaning sound, that never ceased and was, minute by minute, becoming closer, and headed almost straight towards them—they were right in the path of the fire. The big lake was some distance away, across a portage, and there was no time to be lost if they were to cross over to it before the fire rushed down upon them; for, while some forest fires move slowly, others have been known to travel as fast as thirty miles an hour.

As the hot smoke cooled off, it began to come down, settling in a dark, blue haze over all the land, making far-off points invisible and near ones look dim, so that soon nothing could be seen but the row of trees nearest the shore-line, and the children were only able to keep their right direction by watching this, and by the sound of the rapids that lay ahead of them. Very soon they arrived at the head of this steep place in the river, where the water rushed and foamed wildly between, and over, dark jagged rocks for several hundred yards. It was a dangerous place, but Shapian dared not take time, with the double trip they had, to cross the portage that went round it, and he decided to take the quicker route and run the rapids.

For the fire was now not far away, and the sharp turn that he knew to be at the end of the swift water, would head them straight for it. The roar of the fire was now so loud as to almost drown the sound of the noisy rapids, and Shapian soon saw that it was to be a hard race, and a swift one, to gain the lake—and then there was the portage, and it was a long one.

The smoke was now so thick that when they neared the rapids they could not see fifty feet ahead of them, and Shapian had all he could do to find the place to enter it. Standing up in the canoe to get a better view, he at length found the starting point; and then with a swift rush they were into the dashing, boiling white water. Although he was hardly able to see through the smoke, Shapian skilfully picked his way down the crooked, difficult channel between the rocks. Great curling, hissing waves lashed out at the frail canoe, throwing it violently from one white-cap to another; dark, oily-looking swells gripped its underside like evil monsters seeking to pour in over the sides and sink it. Spinning eddies snatched wickedly at the paddles as the little craft leaped like a madly charging horse between the black, savage-looking rocks that lay in wait to rip and tear the light canoe to pieces.

And above the thunderous roar of the tumbling waters there came the duller, deeper, and terribly frightening sound of the oncoming fire. Smoke poured across the river in dense, whirling clouds, and through it sped the leaping canoe with its crew of three. And the sleeping passenger in the basket woke up, and excited by all the noise, and quite aware that something unusual was happening, began to take a part in the proceedings, and added his little thin voice to the uproar, though it could hardly be heard, and he rocked and shook his house of bark so violently that a moment had to be spared to lay a heavy bundle on it to keep it right side up.

Shapian strained and fought with his paddle and all of his young strength against the mighty power of the racing torrent, turning the canoe cleverly this way and that, swinging, sidling, and slipping from one piece of clear water to the next, checking the canoe in the quieter places while he stood up to get a better view of what lay ahead—and then away into the white water again. Meanwhile Sajo pulled and pushed and pried on her paddle with might and main, as Shapian shouted to her above the rattle and the din, "Gyuk-anik" (to the right hand), or "Mashk-anik" (to the left hand), or "Weebetch" (hurry), and sometimes "Pae-ketch" (easy there). Sheets of spray flew from the sides of the canoe as it heaved and bounced and jerked. Some of it came in and Sajo, who was in front, soon became soaked. Except that the smoke made the safe channel so hard to find, they were in no real danger from the rapids itself, for Shapian, like all his people, both young and old, was very skilful in a canoe and understood, even at his age, a great deal about the movements of water; and he had often run this rapids with his father. And Sajo, trusting in him completely, laughed and cried out in her excitement, for this was like a show to her, and she let out little yelps as she had heard her father and the other Indians do, with their louder whoops and yells as they ran a dangerous piece of water—though she had always been left safely on the shore to watch. But Shapian, who knew how serious things really were, never made a sound besides his loud commands as captain of their little ship, and when he could spare an eye from the turmoil of madly boiling water all about him, gave anxious glances to the side from which the fire was coming. And coming it was, with the speed of a train it seemed, rushing down the hills towards them like a crimson sea, with great roaring streamers of flame flying high above the burning forest. Once he looked back, to find that the fire had crossed the narrow lake behind them; now there was only one way to go—forward, though he said never a word to Sajo about it. The air, that had been thick with heavy rolls and banks of smoke, now commenced to turn darker and darker, and the light was dimmed until it appeared almost as though twilight had fallen, so early in the day, and hardly anything could be seen around them; and nothing seemed real any more and they moved like people in a dream.

Desperately Shapian drove the canoe ahead, for well he knew that if they were caught in this place they would be either burnt alive or suffocated. By now the portage was not very far, and beyond it lay the lake that they must get to—and get to fast!

They shot out from the foot of the rapids into a deep, still pool, and here they found themselves surrounded by strange moving shapes, dimly seen through the smoke-clouds, as on all sides all manner of animals were passing, tearing along the shore, or swimming through the pool, or splashing noisily along the shallows, by ones and twos, separately or in small groups, all headed for the big lake, the same one our own travellers were aiming for, each and every one making for the safety he knew that he would find there. Animals that seldom wetted their feet were swimming in the pool—squirrels, rabbits, wood-chucks, and even porcupines. Deer leaped through or over the underbrush, their white tails flashing, eyes wide with terror. A bear lumbered by at a swift, clumsy gallop, and a pair of wolves ran, easily and gracefully, beside a deer—their natural prey; but they never even looked at him. For none were enemies now; no one was hungry, or fierce, or afraid of another. And all the people of the woods, those that went on two legs and others that had four, and those with wings and some that swam, animals and birds and creeping things, creatures, some of them, that dared not meet at any other time, were now fleeing, side by side, from that most merciless of all their foes, dangerous and deadly alike to every one of them from the smallest to the greatest—the Red Enemy of the Wilderness, a forest fire.

Right before the canoe, deep in the water, stood a giant bull moose, largest of all the forest folk, his hair scorched from his back, one of his half-grown horns gone,* his sides heaving as he sucked in great, deep breaths of air; he must have been nearly caught, and perhaps had run many miles with the fire close behind him, and had only escaped because of his enormous strength and speed. Shapian could have touched him with his paddle had he wished, but the huge beast paid them no attention, and getting his wind again, plunged ashore and joined the other creatures of all shapes and sizes that, all brothers now in this great calamity, were hurrying together to the safety of the lake.

And with them, in this wild and queer procession, were our two little Indians and their tiny pet.

Sajo, now realizing what all this meant, became terror-stricken, so Shapian, almost in despair himself, yet knowing that their lives depended on him, kept his courage up and

---

* At the time of this incident, during July, a moose's antlers would be **only** partially developed.

soothed her as best he could, and she paddled bravely on. But the forest that had always been their home, and had always seemed so friendly, had suddenly become a very terrible place to be in. It would have been so to any grown-up; yet these two children, one of them eleven and the other fourteen years of age, remember, kept their heads and fought like good soldiers for their lives, and for Chilawee's. And this same Chilawee was no great help, as you can well believe; on the contrary, he showed every sign of causing trouble and delay. Sensing real danger, as all animals do, and scared out of his wits by the sounds and scent of the other creatures that passed on every side, he was screeching at the top of his lungs and pounding and tearing at the lid of his prison, as it must now have seemed to him, and if some way were not found to quiet him, he would soon be out of it; and once in the water he could never again be found in all this hurry and confusion.

A few short minutes and they were at the portage. The trail was nearly hidden by the blinding smoke, and down the slopes of the nearby ridge the hoarse roar of the fire was coming swiftly. The darkness that had fallen as the smoke poured over the forest, was now lighted up by a terrible red glow, and the heat from it could be plainly felt. Quickly they threw their stuff ashore. Chilawee was now in such a state that he could never be carried in any other way except as a separate load. This landing being safe for the minute, and not knowing what shape things were in at the other end, they at once decided to leave him here. It was but the work of a moment to turn the canoe over on top of the basket, so as to hold down the lid (like all his

kind when very frightened, Chilawee forgot to use his teeth),
and taking each a load the children started across, running at a
dog-trot.* On all sides thick moving coils of black and yellow
smoke wound and billowed around them as they ran, took
strange shapes and forms and seemed to reach out with pale
waving hands to hold them back. Through the whirling smoke-
clouds the trees beside the trail loomed indistinct like tall, dark,
silent ghosts; while here and there red eyes of flame glowed at
them through the haze.

But Sajo and Shapian kept right on at their steady trot. At
the far side there was a breeze from off the lake, and the end of
the portage was clear. Gulping a few breaths of fresh air, they
left their loads beside the waters' edge and raced back for Chilawee and the canoe. The race was often little but a scramble as,
gasping and half-blinded, they staggered down the trail, half
the time with their eyes closed to relieve the pain in them, and
to shut out the stinging, burning smoke, while they groped their
way along, their hearts filled with a fear such as they had never
before known. By the time they were back at the canoe, sparks
and burning brands were falling everywhere, and the angry
glow had deepened so that everything, trees, smoke, and water,
were red with it. And now, close at hand, could be heard a
dreadful, low, rushing sound.

The fire was almost upon them.

And at the same time Chilawee, having made up his mind
to save his own little life as best he could, was gnawing steadily

---

* This is not an unusual pace with Indians when carrying a load, and on level
ground is easier than walking.

away at the thin bark sides of his box; in no time at all he would be through. If only it would hold together for just five more minutes!

In a moment Shapian tore off his sister's head shawl, and quickly soaking it in water, with swift movements wrapped it about her head and face, leaving only her eyes and nose showing. Then splashing water over her clothes, he said:

"Do not wait. I will come quickly. Go!"

And hugging Chilawee's basket tight to her body with both arms, Sajo disappeared into that awful, glowing tunnel of a trail.

X

THE EMPTY BASKET

AFTER he had seen his sister pass from sight, Shapian was delayed perhaps a full minute while he wetted his own clothes and slipped the paddles into the carrying-thongs. How he wished now for his father's guiding hand! He was doing the best he knew, with his small experience, to save the lives of all three of them (for he looked on the little beaver almost as though he, too, were a person, a little brother who must be saved as well) and he hoped he had chosen aright. And now Sajo was in there ahead of him, alone; he must hurry!

Throwing the canoe up, and over, with his head inside between the paddles, which formed a kind of yoke, he was quickly on his way. But in that short minute that he had been detained, the fire had gained on him, and while he ran as swiftly as a boy of fourteen could well do with a twelve-foot canoe on his shoulders, he saw, not far away to one side, a solid, crackling wall of flame. Trees fell crashing in the midst of it, and others burst with loud reports like gun-fire. Onward he tore through what had now become a cave of crimson smoke, half-choked, his eyes stinging, his head throbbing with the heat. But he clenched his teeth and kept on, while close beside him the blazing forest crackled, and thundered, and roared. Whole tree-tops caught fire with a rush and a horrible screeching, tearing sound, and flames leaped from tree to tree like fiery banners, ever nearer and nearer to the trail.

Beneath the canoe some clear air remained, which helped him

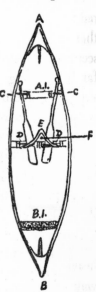

A. Bow.

A.1. Bow Seat.

B. Stern.

B.1. Stern Seat.

C.C. Thongs Holding Paddles in Place.

D.D. Thongs Holding Blades of Paddles.

E. Head-Strap.

F. Person's head and shoulders go here, head-strap fitting over their head, and the blades of the paddles resting on the shoulders, the canoe being upside down.

The thongs *C.C.* and *D.D.* are never untied, the paddles being pushed in or out of them, under the head-strap.

A twelve-foot bark canoe would weigh about thirty-five pounds.

INDIAN METHOD OF CARRYING A CANOE

a little, but the heat was all he could stand. Once a burning spruce tree came crashing down so near the portage that its flaming top fell across the trail ahead of him in a flurry of sparks and licking tongues of flame, and he was obliged to wait precious moments while the first fury of the burning brush died down. Then he jumped, with the canoe still on his shoulders, over the glowing trunk. The hot breath of it fanned his body and nearly strangled him, and he stumbled to his knees as he landed. Righting himself he cleared the canoe before the fire had harmed it, but the bravely flying fox tail had caught on fire, and in a moment was scorched to a crisp. But he went on.

On the upturned canoe fell large flakes of burning bark and red-hot ashes, that lay there and smoked and smouldered, so that to any one who might have followed him, it must have seemed to be already burning, which for very truth, it was not far from doing. And now he should have caught up to his sister; she would be slower than he, for the basket was an awkward affair to run with, whereas a bark canoe, though very much heavier, was a steady, well-balanced load, even for a boy. And he suddenly became terrified lest Chilawee had cut open his box and escaped on the way, and that Sajo having delayed somewhere to capture him, he had passed them. But just ahead, the smoke was clearing and he felt the wind from the lake. Then, sick and dizzy, his sight blurred by the water that streamed from his eyes, he stumbled again, and this time fell heavily, canoe and all, over something soft that lay in the pathway—there, face down across the trail, lay Sajo! And clutched tightly in one of her hands was the basket—empty. Chilawee had at last cut his way out, and was gone!

Hardly knowing what he was doing, Shapian crawled from under the canoe, lifted Sajo across his knees, scrambled, somehow, to his feet and then, his breath coming in choking sobs, his knees bending under him and a great ringing in his ears, he staggered with her in his arms to the lake shore.

Here he laid her down and threw water over her face, and rubbed her hands, and cried out, "Sajo, Sajo, speak to me, speak!" And she opened her eyes and said faintly, "Chilawee." And he dared not tell her there was no Chilawee any more, only an empty basket.

And now the smoke was rolling out over them even here; the whole portage was aflame, and waiting only to wet Sajo's shawl and throw it over her face, Shapian went back for the canoe. Fortunately it was not far, as, unable to lift it any more, he seized it by one end and dragged it to the water, stern out and bow inshore so as to load the quicker. Quickly he threw in the bundles, and lifted Sajo into the bow, while she held tightly to the basket and cried weakly, "Chilawee, Chilawee, Chilawee," and moaned, and kept repeating, "Chilawee."

All this took but a short time, and running lightly over the load to the other end, Shapian commenced to back the canoe out stern first, as fast as he was able and a big sob came in his throat as he thought of their little furry friend who was now past all help. Yet surely, he thought, the little creature, gifted to find water easily, might have reached the lake, and even if lost might still be living—when, behind him, from out on the lake, came the sound of a smart slap, and a splash upon the water, and there was the lost Chilawee, alive and quite well, thank you, giving out, by means of his tail, his private and personal opinion of this Red Enemy that he had so narrowly escaped. And Shapian shouted out in a great voice, "Sajo! Sajo! Chilawee is safe, Chilawee is out on the lake—look!"

And at that Sajo, lying there in the bow of the canoe, burst into tears and sobbed as if her heart would break; she would not cry before, when she believed her little friend was dead, but now he was known to be safe she was free to cry all she wanted, to cry as loud and as long as she liked—with joy!

Chilawee was quite far out, and in no danger, but a canoe does not start very quickly when paddled backwards, and being still in shallow water, was too close to shore for safety; and at the edge of the forest, leaning out over the water, was a huge pine tree that was hollow, and had been burning firecely all this time. Shapian was still struggling to get the canoe backed away far enough to turn it (and it did not take nearly as long for all this to happen as it does to tell about it), when the bark of the pine, dried out by the intense heat, cracked wide open, and the hurrying tongues of fire rushed up this channel as if it had been a stove-pipe, to the top of it. The great fan-shaped head of the towering tree, that had looked proudly out over the wilderness for many a hundred years, burst into a mass of flame that leaped into the air above it, the height again of the tree itself. And then the burnt-out butt, unable to stand against the force of the soaring flames, gave way, and the mighty trunk tottered and began to fall, outwards towards the lake, swayed a little sideways, and then started on its fiery path, straight for the canoe. Slowly at first, then faster and faster the hundred-foot giant overbalanced, and the terrible fan of flame rushed downwards. Real terror, for the first time, seized on Shapian, and with desperate strength he stopped the canoe and drove it smashing into the shore, while just behind him the burning tree plunged into the lake with a deafening crash, and a hissing and a screeching that could have been heard for a mile or more as the fire and water met. Smoke and steam poured up and

"A BURNING TREE CRASHED DOWN INTO THE TRAIL IN FRONT OF HIM" Go.

smothered everything as the flames went out, so that Shapian could see nothing, and the waves from this terrific splash rocked the canoe violently and Sajo, beside herself with fright, jumped to her feet in the dangerously rolling canoe and screamed, and screamed, and Shapian sprang over the side and ran through the water to her, and held her in his arms, and comforted her, and told her that there was nothing more to fear.

And out on the lake Master Chilawee slapped his little tail in small defiance; or perhaps it was intended for an imitation of the falling tree—in which case, I can tell you that it was a pretty feeble imitation.

In a few short moments the canoe was away, this time without any accident, and the little beaver, seeming mighty glad that he was found again, gave himself up quite cheerfully and was lifted by this so impudent tail of his and dropped aboard, where he clambered around on the load, and smelled at the children, and ran about, and altogether showed signs of the greatest pleasure and excitement. He did not seem to have lost one single hair, no doubt because he ran so low to the ground on his short legs, so that everything passed over him; and so now he was celebrating, and they all had quite a reunion out there on the lake.

Before they had gone very far, Sajo began to feel better, and soon was well enough to sit up. Shapian would not let her paddle, and had her sit facing him, while she told her story, and related how, choked by the hot, burning smoke, and not being able to see, she had been unable to catch Chilawee when he fell from the basket, and had become confused and fallen, where, she did not know, and had then been unable to get up again. And that was all she knew about it until she found Shapian pouring water over her face. She did not remember calling Chilawee, though she knew he had run away, having seen him, as in a dream, disappear into the clouds of smoke. And when she was done her story she began to look hard at her brother's face, and then to laugh! And the more she looked the louder she laughed, and Shapian was a little frightened, and began to wonder if the dangers she had been through had touched her mind, until she exclaimed:

"Shapian!—your face—you should see it, why—you have no eyebrows!" And then suddenly she stopped laughing and felt for her own eyebrows, and asked anxiously: "How are mine, are they all right?" and looked over the side of the canoe at the water to see the reflection of her face. But the canoe was moving, and ruffling the water and she could, of course, see nothing, and now very alarmed, she cried:

"Oh, stop the canoe so I can see—tell me, are my eyebrows there?" And she got into a great way about it, and Shapian laughed at her, in his turn, and would not say; until at last he told her they were there all right, yes, both of them; which indeed they were, as her face had been covered most of the time. But it was just like a girl, said Shapian to himself, to worry about a little thing like eyebrows when they had all so nearly lost their lives. And truly, a little more, and there would have been no happy ending to *this* story.

The canoe had suffered most and was leaking rather badly, but otherwise everything was going quite smoothly again. But behind them the fire swept over the portage and on beyond it, like a conquering army, leaving everything in its path a blackened, smoking ruin. Well, they were safe now, and except for two aching heads and two pairs of smarting eyes, were in the best of spirits. Shapian, for once, felt quite encouraged at having beaten the fire, because, as Sajo put it, there was hardly *anything* worse to be met with than a forest fire, and they had come right *through* it (as she imagined), so nothing in the world could *ever* keep them now from Chikanee. And as for Chilawee, he appeared to have come through the affair the best of any of them, and evidently gave the matter no further thought, and stretching himself out on the bottom of the canoe, with his head comfortably pillowed on Sajo's knee, he promptly went to sleep.

That afternoon they made an early camp, in a good safe place, on an island far out on the lake, and here they looked over the damage. Shapian could not very well repair his eyebrows, which would grow out later of their own accord, but he had plenty to do with the canoe. The gay and gallant tail was just a blackened, shrivelled piece of skin, and the once keen and watchful eye was nearly gone, most of the paint having blistered, and cracked, and fallen off. The hard smash the bow had got against the shore when they had dodged the falling tree, had torn off a good-sized strip of bark; the spruce gum at the seams had melted, and the burning embers that had fallen on it had smouldered long enough to scorch a number of thin places in the sides and bottom. Also their tent and blankets had a few holes burnt in them by flying sparks. But the loss was quite small, considering, and they could easily have fared a great deal worse. The top was gone from Chilawee's box, and in the side of it was a hole the size of a quart measure, Chilawee's part in the battle! But there were plenty of birch trees around, and Shapian cut sheets of bark from them, and sewed a patch on the hole and made another lid that fitted nearly as well as the old one, and he fixed up the canoe with a few patches and some fresh gum. The eye and the tail would have to wait until later. Sajo, meanwhile, busied herself with needle and thread, which no Indian girl or woman will travel very far without, and soon had the tent and blankets serviceable again, and by the time darkness fell, everything was in readiness for a new start in the morning.

And that night, as the two of them sat side by side, looking across to the mainland, they were thinking how nearly they had come to never seeing their father again, and they were lonesome for him. And they could hear, even yet, faintly in the distance, the low moaning of the fire, while the sky shone red for many miles, lit up by the beautiful, but terrible glow from that greatest of all dangers of the wilderness, before whom all alike are helpless, and which can be brought about so easily so that great forests, and thousands of animals, and often whole townsful of people, have been destroyed by a single match in the hands of one careless man.

And later, as Shapian lay on his bed of brush, watching the slow fading of the red glow on the canvas walls of the tent, as the fire died down amongst the swamps and bare rocks that it finally had a run into, he came to the very pleasing conclusion that even if he were not really yet a man, at this rate of going, it would not be very long before he was one.

And looking over at Sajo, who lay fast asleep with Chilawee cuddled in her arms, he heaved a big sigh, and closing his eyes, was soon with them in the Land of Dreams.

XI

WHITE BROTHER TO THE INDIANS

AFTER two more days of travel, Sajo and Shapian arrived at Rabbit Portage. Its full name was Wapoose-ka-neemeech,* or in English, The Place of Dancing Rabbits. It had been so named because rabbits were very thick at this place some years, and these animals have a way of thumping their hind feet rapidly on the ground, so that by moonlight, when there are a number of them doing this, it appears and sounds very much as if they were dancing. However, I think we will call it Rabbit Portage, as the white people do.

The youngsters pitched their camp in a little bay near the post, where Chilawee could swim in safety, as the regular Indian camping ground, though empty just now, would be swarming with hungry sleigh dogs that had to find their living as best they could in the Summer time, and would kill anything that was small enough, and eat anything that was not made of wood or iron; even very young children had to be kept out of their way. After the tent was up, and a good thick, springy floor of brush laid down, and wood had been collected and everything comfortably stowed in its place, Shapian took the canoe and went to visit the fur-post.

* Pronounced *Wah*-poose-kah-*nee*-meech.

Here he found the trader, the same trader who had been to their home on that fateful day, earlier in the Summer. He was new to the country and could talk only a little Indian, and Shapian's English was not any too good. So the trader took him into his little private office behind the store, where they would not be interrupted, and here they managed somehow to understand one another. Shapian, standing before the trader upright as an arrow, explained everything as best he could. He told how everything had seemed to go wrong since Chikanee had been sold, and how his sister was all the time downhearted, and how lonesome was Chilawee, and how unhappy they all were. And the trader, sitting there behind his desk, looking more like a judge than a trader, listened very closely to all that Shapian said, and when he had finished the white man said:

"So Chila—who—?"

"Chilawee," corrected Shapian.

"Oh, yes," continued the trader, looking very severe, "so Chikalee, he's lonesome, eh? And your sister too; and you want Chik—what's his name again?—Chinawee back, eh?"

"Yes," answered Shapian patiently. "Want Chikanee back."

And the trader cleared his throat rather gruffly, and gave a little snort—what nonsense, he thought, so much fuss over a little whining beast no bigger than a puppy! But Shapian kept on in a low, even voice, picking his words slowly and carefully in the trader's language, of which he knew so little:

"Me, I will work. I will make wood [he meant "cut wood"] for your Winter. I work all Summer for you; also I sell you my gun. So I trade now, the wood and my gun for Chikanee. Those are my words, me." But they were words that trembled a little at the last, for this gun was very dear to him.

"I don't want your gun," said the trader sharply. "This post sold it to you, and we most certainly won't buy it back. This is no pawnshop!" And his hard blue eyes looked very fierce indeed. Poor Shapian, who didn't even know what a pawnshop was, looked down at his moccasins to hide the trembling of his lips, and then proudly raised his head again, and said in his low voice:

"Then I work all Winter as well, me: all one year I work for you. One year for Chikanee."

Fiddlesticks! thought the trader, was the boy crazy? It was plain to be seen that this man knew very little about Indians. Suddenly he asked:

"Did you see the fire?"

"Yes," replied Shapian. "Me, Sajo, Chilawee, pass through fire; one portage burning up. Pretty near finish us."

The white man stared hard at him—through the fire! "Preposterous," he was about to say, and was going to speak roughly again; but he thought the better of it, and made only another gruff sound in his throat. For even he could not help seeing how much in earnest the little fellow was; and then, seeing this, he was really sorry, for he knew that he could do nothing. Chikanee had been sold again, this time to some city people who had a park where wild beasts were kept in cages (Chikanee a wild beast!), and a live beaver was a rare and valuable animal. He explained all this to Shapian, still speaking roughly because he

"I DON'T WANT YOUR GUN"
SAID THE TRADER, SHARPLY.

was new to trading and thought that it was the right way to speak to Indians, though in spite of his red, angry face and hard blue eyes, he was not quite the ogre he made himself out to be, and he finished by feeling the least bit uncomfortable. And he talked in as kindly a tone as he was able to, when he told Shapian that Chikanee (Chikaroo this time!) had been gone a month now, and had been sold for fifty dollars.

Fifty dollars! The boy's heart sank—fifty dollars, he had never seen such a sum. Traders hardly ever gave money; they gave only goods in exchange for fur, because the Indians would only have to spend the money in the same store they got it from in the first place, at the post, so it was hardly worth the trouble of carrying around. Fifty dollars—his offer of work, and his precious gun, both refused! And he had nothing else to give. But it was not his way to give up quickly, and he went back to camp and told Sajo that he had found out just where Chikanee was. And she was very glad at this piece of news; for he never told her how hard-hearted the trader had been, nor about the large sum of money that they would never be able to get. So Sajo thought that there was nothing to do now but wait until Shapian had cut a little wood, and earned their fare to the city and back (it couldn't be very much, people came and went every few days!), and a little besides to buy back Chikanee with. And in a way she was right, that was all there was to do. But she didn't know how hopeless it all really was.

So Shapian bore his load of misery alone, and racked his young brains to think of a way to earn fifty dollars. And as for the railroad fare, he had been afraid to even ask about it, and sometimes, too, he wondered what his father was going to say about all this, though he was pretty sure that anything he did to make Sajo happy, would be very easily forgiven, even if it were not quite what had been expected of him. All night he tossed and turned in his blanket while he planned and planned. If only they could get to the city somehow! He had heard that some of these white people were kind, especially the city people; not at all like the traders. If he could get down there and tell the folks who owned Chikanee, how things were and how miserable everybody was, perhaps they would let Chikanee go home with Sajo, while he stayed behind and worked for them till the little prisoner's freedom had been paid for. Otherwise, he was sure, the whole expense would come to a hundred dollars. Poor Shapian, he could think of no greater amount of money than a hundred dollars. He had heard spoken of as rich, an Indian who had earned a hundred dollars real money; this man had been out as a forest guide with a party of Americans. These Gitchie Mokoman—Big Knives, as the Indians called the Americans, were not hard to work for; they expected their guides to be friends, not servants, so the men of the village said, and they paid very high wages and often gave away their tents, or blankets, or guns, even whole camping outfits, after the trip was over. And at that thought a new idea came to him; and it was this:

Every second or third day, there came up river to Rabbit Portage a big, clumsy-looking steamboat, a wood burner with two decks and huge wheels on its sides, in boxes. This unlikely-looking craft made the journey back and forth to the railroad.

But no one could go aboard without money—always money, thought Shapian, and wondered how much the captain wanted for the trip; more money than he had, anyway, for he had none at all. But numbers of Americans came up on the boat from time to time. It was quite likely that some of them would need a guide, and this was work that he was well able to do.* Full of this fresh plan, he hurried over to the post as soon as he had had his breakfast; but there was no one there except the trader until nearly noon, when the steamer was expected. Shortly before mid-day this cumbersome affair chugged its way up the river and came in to the dock in a grand sweeping half circle with a great splashing of paddle-wheels, and shouting of orders, and bell-ringing, and all the pomp and circumstance to be expected of the one and only real, live steamboat in the entire country. Sure enough, a crowd of tourists came ashore with their camping outfits, each having enough, to Shapian's notion, to supply at least forty people. They looked curiously at the Indian boy, with his buckskin moccasins and long braided hair, the first real Indian that some of them had ever seen, and they whispered and passed remarks amongst themselves, and one or two pointed black boxes towards him and clicked them at him. And he was ashamed and shy in front of all these people, who were so noisy, who dressed so strangely, and whose faces were either so very red or very pale. And suddenly he felt very small and very much alone before them all, and he knew that

* The hunting, fishing and scenic beauties of Northern Canada have attracted to the more accessible outposts large numbers of sportsmen, largely Americans, who employ the Indians as guides, or scouts, and some of the villages derive their sole revenue from this source.

never could he be brave enough to guide even one of them; and he turned and commenced to walk away as fast as he possibly could, without actually running, when he heard a voice calling out in Indian,

"Wait, my son, wait. I want to speak with you."

He had seen no Indians there, but he stopped, and looking back, saw coming towards him some one who was speaking in the Ojibway language quite as well as he did himself, yet who was not an Indian at all, but a white man, tall and strong looking, with bright yellow hair and blue eyes—not hard blue eyes such as the post manager had, but smiling, kind blue eyes. His white shirt was open at the throat, and his sleeves were rolled up above his elbows, all of his skin that showed was tanned by the sun, almost to the same colour as an Indian's. And he wore moccasins; though Shapian, in spite of his nervousness, noticed that he walked a little carefully in them,* as though he was not very well used to them. And the stranger came close to him and put his hand on the boy's shoulder, and somehow, Shapian was no more shy or awkward, and he paid no more attention to the loudly talking tourists who were watching, and saw only the smiling brown face, and heard only the words of this fairhaired man who spoke his language so well, using all the soft tones that Shapian was so accustomed to.

"Do not be afraid," said the yellow-haired man. (Shapian had already named him Yellow Hair, in his own mind.) "These are all good people, Gitchie Mokoman—Americans. They like

---

* The word "tenderfoot" arose from the inability of newcomers in the wilderness to wear moccasins until their feet became hardened to their use.

Indians, and only want to take your picture." Just the same he drew Shapian away, as he went on: "But let us go to your camp and talk. I want to hear about your adventure in the fire, and besides, I have wished to see the children of Gitchie Meegwon this long time." He said that he knew Big Feather very well, calling him Quill, as all the white people did.

Shapian felt right away that this was a friend, and his heart warmed toward the man, and although he had known him only so short a time, he felt that here, at last, was some one he could trust. And so he led his new friend through the woods to the camp, not taking him in the canoe, as he had always heard that a white man would upset you in so small a canoe— though he afterwards found out that this brown young man could handle a canoe very well indeed.

Sajo had been getting dinner ready, but when she saw them coming she ran and hid herself in the tent, for, besides the trader, whom she hated, she had never seen a white man so close before, and Shapian found that he was going to have quite a job to coax her out of there. But when she heard the visitor talking Indian so well, and heard his merry laugh, she peeped out, and found herself looking fair and square into the kindest and merriest pair of eyes, next to her father's, she had ever seen —and then she knew she was caught, and so came out, and sat by the fire and pretended to be extremely busy with the pots and dishes. Just the same, she wanted very much to look at this so very pleasant stranger, and so she pulled her head shawl well over her face, and peeped out at him from under it. And every so often he would catch her at it, and she would blush and bob her head down, so the shawl hid her face again, and would get so busy around the fire that at last there really was some cooking done. And so they all had dinner together. And Shapian felt for this white man even more respect, when he found that he could seat himself on the ground as comfortably as any Indian, something that Shapian had so far never seen any white man able to do, except the trappers, who are often, themselves, very like Indians in their ways.

And the yellow-haired man praised the cooking, and said he had not enjoyed such a meal for a long time; and I don't really think he had, for it had only been bannock, with lard instead of butter, and some strips of dried deer meat, and tea without any sugar. From the way he acted, you would never have known but that it was a feast.

After dinner, their guest lit a cigarette and smoked a while. Sajo found this to be a very strange way of smoking. All the Indians, including a good many of the old women, used pipes, and she had never seen a cigarette used before; but she supposed it was another strange idea of this strange man, who talked such good Indian and yet had such queer ways about him—but mighty pleasant ways, they agreed together in whispers.

And while he smoked the stranger told them about himself. He was a missionary, not—he put in hastily—one of the interfering kind that wanted to change *all* the Indian customs and simple beliefs, some of which he thought were very beautiful; nor did he want to force his own particular way upon them, but he was one who felt towards them as a brother. He had learned the Indian language from books, and moved from place to place amongst the Bush Crees, the Salteaux,* the Algonquins and Ojibways (all of whom talk a similar language), working amongst them, teaching school, taking care of the sick, and trying to bring happiness wherever he could. And all because he felt that all the people of the world belonged to one great family, and believed that the Great Spirit loved and cared equally well for both red men and white, and he wanted to work for Him. And he told them how there were good people in the cities who paid all his expenses so that he was able to give his full time to this work, without having to ask the Indians for anything.

And this Indian boy and girl listened in wonder to hear such things, for they had always supposed that the Indians had been forgotten, and that no one cared any more about what happened to them, now that their land had been gotten away from them. But they could not help but believe that this man was what he said, a brother to them, even though his skin did show to be so very white wherever the sun had not touched it, and though his eyes were not black like theirs, but blue as the sky itself at noon-day.

About this time Chilawee, who had been drying himself off after his latest bath and combing himself in the tent, hearing all the talking, and having, I suspect, more than an inkling that something was going on in the way of dinner, now came tumbling out to see what it was all about. Seeing the stranger, he at once decided that he must be examined. On his way over he came to the dinner table, which was nothing but a clean, white sheet of canvas laid upon the ground, with the dinner

* Pronounced Soto.

things still on it, and he walked right across this, tramping among the dishes, until he arrived in front of the visitor, and he then sat up on his hind legs and took a good close look at him. Perhaps he thought that such a large visitor ought to be good for quite a lot of bannock, if properly handled—anyhow, what he saw seemed to please him very much, for he commenced to shake his head back and forth, and from side to side and shook his body, quite in his old way of dancing, and presently fell on his back among the dishes where he continued to squirm and wiggle. And there was a magnificent clatter, and a great upsetting, and a spilling, and a scatteration of cups and plates, so, to quiet things down Sajo hurriedly gave him a big chunk of bannock, expecting him to go back in the tent to eat it. But this time he was not to be so easily bribed to leave the company, and he squatted right there on the tablecloth, and taking his bannock in both hands, commenced to enjoy himself thoroughly—keeping one bright black eye on the visitor.

And this was the first time since Chikanee had gone away that he had done his funny dance; so that Sajo took it for a sign, and was more sure than ever that things were going to work out for the best. Yellow Hair, for his part, thought this performance was about the funniest thing he had ever seen, and laughed so heartily that Sajo, quite forgetting to be bashful, joined in, for it certainly was a most comical sight, and even Shapian, for all his heavy heart, could not help but laugh a little too.

Then Yellow Hair asked them how they came to have a beaver, which is the shyest of all animals, so tame, though he already knew quite a lot about it from the trader; and he asked them many more questions. And although they were not, at first, very willing to tell him, he at last got all the story (for he was very clever at questions, this young man), how the two little beavers had been saved when they were nearly ready to die, and how they had been a birthday gift to Sajo from her father, and how they came to be named Chilawee and Chikanee —Big Small and Little Small. And he heard how sad they all had been since Little Small had been taken away from them, and how unhappy and lonesome poor Chilawee had become, and he listened (he was a very good listener too) while they told how they had started out to search for their little friend, and on the way had nearly lost their lives in the forest fire. And Shapian, at the end, said that he must now find ·work so as to have money to go to the city and bring Chikanee home again.

And after he had heard it all, the young man looked grave and became very quiet, and the laughter was quite gone from off his face; for he knew that there was no work for Shapian, though he kept it to himself. And he reached out thoughtfully and stroked the soft, silky fur of the little beaver and said, half to himself, in English,

"So this is Big Small; and Little Small is far away, alone in the city. And these children—this must not be!"

And he stole a glance at Sajo, for he had noticed her pull her shawl, which had fallen across her shoulders, back over her head again; and he could see beneath it, two big tears rolling slowly down her cheeks, though she had tried very hard to keep them back.

So he arose, and went away. But before he left he said to them:

"I am your friend, and your father's friend. Tomorrow I will return, and we will have dinner together again. Perhaps I can take away this cloud that lies so dark across your trail. I do not know, but I will try very hard. That is my work, to help clear away the mists from the face of the sun, that it may shine upon us all."

And with a wave of his hand he was gone.

XII

The Big Knives

IMMEDIATELY after his return to the post, the missionary had a long talk with the trader in his office. Soon he came out with a sheet of paper marked "NOTICE," which he tacked on the door of the building. The tourists were still around at that time of the day, and several of them saw him doing this, and right away they all had to see what was on the notice. It called every one to a meeting that was to be held, at four o'clock, in the Indian schoolhouse on the hill behind the store, on a matter of great importance. In so small a place the news quickly spread, and, having nothing better to do, and rather wondering what this busy-appearing fellow might have to say, everybody that could go, went.

The room was small, and some had to stand outside, listening in at the windows and the door. The young man with the yellow hair stood upon the teacher's platform, and when every one was settled he commenced to speak. At first you could hear a little whispering, and coughing, and shuffling of feet, but this soon died down as he went on, and soon everybody was listening, listening very hard. For he was telling the people a tale; something very different from what they had expected, something such as they had never heard before. He was as good at tales as he was at questions, this White Brother to the

Indians. And the place became very quiet; and there was no sound but that of the young man's voice.

And the tale he told was the story of Sajo and Shapian, of Big Small and Little Small.

And at the last he said:

". . . for we are still our brother's keeper. And let us remember that these young people who have braved the dangers of the Wilderness as perhaps you and I could not have done, whose colour is perhaps different to ours, whose language is not our language, and whose ways are not our ways, are *our* responsibility, yours and mine; they are not just a couple of Indian kids, but two very unhappy children. And who knows but what they may be right in what they think, and that those small beasts that are their friends may have, after all, feelings that are very like our own.

"And let me say, before you go, that as you pass out through the door you will find, on the right, a large, empty Hudson's Bay tea-can; it will hold about a quart. How about it, folks?"

When he had finished, the place broke out into a kind of a mild uproar, and everybody seemed to want to speak at once, and the ladies were saying: "Oh! Did you ever hear—" and "Imagine, all that way alone!" and "—poor dears, through that dreadful fire!" And gentlemen stood up and reached into their pockets, and talked loudly to one another, and made such remarks as, "Why, I wouldn't have missed this for anything," and "Where are they; we've got to do something about it." And one of them asked: "Where did he say the can was?"

And as the people commenced to file out through the door

there came, from the direction of the tea-can, cheerful clinking sounds, and the crackle of crisp new bills and the rustle of old ones; and not all one-dollar bills either, let me tell you, but twos, and fives, and the odd ten as well. And there were, besides, young people who wanted to help, and these too put in whatever they could spare from their holiday allowances.

And last of all the trader went out; and when he came to the door he looked carefully around to make sure that no one was looking, winked one eye (the one farthest from the tea-can), and reaching out quickly as though he were afraid of being seen, dropped into the can a tightly folded little wad of bills, and was heard to mutter to himself:

"Well, Chikawee, or Chilakee, or Chikalee, or whatever you call yourself, here's good luck to you!"

But this brown young man, who was still on the platform, was not only good at questions and answers, and at telling stories; he also had remarkably good eyesight. And *he* saw.

Later in the day Yellow Hair went over to the children's camp, and when Shapian saw all that money, he could hardly believe it was for him. He was even a little frightened, and asked:

"What must I do—what work do they want me to do?"

"Nothing," answered Yellow Hair. "There is no time to work. You must go at once, or perhaps your little friend will be gone—animals get so lonely they sometimes die. These Gitchie Mokoman, they say for me to tell you that it is a gift. Long ago, the nation to which they belong was very cruel to the Indians, and they know now that wrong was done, and they

are sorry; now they want to help. They are a great and generous people. All they ask is, that sometime, when you meet
some one in trouble, help them if you can."

"Oh! I will, I will," said Shapian earnestly. "Tell them I
will, and that I thank them." The tears stood in his eyes, where
all his troubles had never been able to bring them. And so the
roll of money was placed carefully in an envelope, while Sajo
looked on, her eyes big and round with joy, and excitement,
and about half a dozen other feelings that she would never have
been able to tell you about; she knew nothing whatever about
money, but now, she thought, there was nothing between them
and Chikanee, nothing at all. She was glad, but not a bit surprised, and she said she had just *known* that everything was
going to be all right, and that the white people were not *nearly*
as bad as they were made out to be, and that it only went to
show how true her dream had been!

In the envelope the Yellow Hair enclosed a note to the station
agent at the railroad station, asking for two return tickets to
the city. And although this looked like nearly all the money
in the world to Shapian, after the railroad fares were paid there
would be very little left; for, although the tourists had been
generous, there had not been, after all, very many of them.
The missionary thought to himself that perhaps Shapian might
have to stay behind and work out the price of Chikanee's liberty, if the park owners would consider such a thing. Anyhow,
the only thing to do was to try. Yellow Hair also gave Shapian
a letter addressed to the head man of the group of workers to
which he belonged, who would find lodgings for them, and

told him that as soon as he arrived in the city he should ask to be taken to a policeman, and then show him the address on the envelope. The missionary explained very carefully what a policeman looked like and how he would be dressed, and made Shapian practise saying the word. The nearest he got to it was "poliss-man"; but this was considered to be quite plain enough to be understood. Chikanee, he told them, had been sold to the owner of an amusement park in the city, and any policeman could take them there.

And now, thought Shapian, with any luck at all, they should be back in time to welcome their father home, as the brigade was expected to return soon; and, he reflected, it was a lot easier to explain things when something you did, that was a little against the rules, turned out to be all to the good.

Their friend helped them to collect a bundle of poplar feed for Chilawee, besides the bannock that Sajo had made, and he promised to take care of their canoe and camping outfit until they should return. And when, on the following day, the boat was ready to leave, everybody in the whole place was on the dock to see them off. Some of the American ladies had fallen right in love with little Sajo, calling her Brown Eyes, and Little Moccasins, and one of them named her Madame Butterfly. And the men shook hands with Shapian all around, and called him a brave fellow, and said they were proud to know him. Even Chilawee came in for his share of the attention, though I don't believe he liked it very well, for he turned his back on folks in a manner that was decidedly impolite, and carried on with his own small affairs. The trader was there, looking around very severely, as if he heartily disapproved of the whole business; for he was determined that no one should ever know that he had put any money into this ridiculous affair.

At the very last, the missionary, who had been standing apart from the crowd looking at the trader, smiling to himself about something or another, came to the gangplank just as Sajo and Shapian walked aboard, and took the hand of each of them, and patted the little beaver on the nose, and said:

"Good luck to you, children of Gitchie Meegwon. I will tell your father everything. May you be successful, and all four of you come safely home again. We will be waiting."

.   .   .   .

That very day, three canoes could be seen approaching the burnt portage on which Sajo, Shapian, and Chilawee had had their desperate adventure. The canoes came onward at terrific speed. In them were Indians, stripped to the waist, their long hair tied out of the way in knots on top of their heads. Silent, grim-looking men they were, their naked shoulders glistening with the sweat of hard paddling. The brown bodies bent and swayed and paddles flashed in the sunlight as the canoes drove down swiftly upon the portage. The first one had no more than touched land, when a man leaped ashore. It was Big Feather. The brigade had returned and Big Feather had found his cabin empty!

Throwing himself on his knees beside the water he scraped away the litter of the fire, now cold, and found there the sharp

V made by the bow of a canoe; and he saw, too, a small moccasin track, half washed away. Springing to his feet he shouted:

"They have passed here. Quickly! Take axes, clean out the portage, I will search the trail for—" He stopped as an old man with white hair and a wise, wrinkled face, said:

"Stay, my son. My old eyes have seen many things. Stay and rest yourself. *I* will first cross the trail. Perhaps I may read——"

And Gitchie Meegwon bowed his head to the words of his Chief, and waited, patiently. The trail was piled high with blackened, twisted trees, criss-crossed in every direction. The men chopped furiously amongst the fallen timber to open a passage for the canoes, while Gitchie Meegwon, unable to rest, busied himself cooking for the others, for the work would take no little time.

The old man went on across the portage, and searched very carefully amongst the wreckage of the fire, for whatever there might be of tracks or other traces of the children. As we know, he found no little bodies, but any logs that lay flat on the ground, and that he was able to move, he lifted aside, and looked beneath them very closely for tracks or any other signs. For fire sometimes moves so quickly that it leaves its work half done in places; and under one of these fallen logs, crushed but only partly burnt, he found the top of Chilawee's basket. He found, too, at the far end, a deep cut in the soft soil of the landing, where a canoe must have been driven very violently ashore—why? he asked himself, when it was going the other way! And then, looking out shrewdly at the huge tree, half burnt, that lay in the water no more than the length of two canoes away, he read the story to himself. For he was a very wise old man, and had been a warrior once, in days gone by, and could read the Wilderness as we read a book. And for this he had been named Ne-Ganik-Abo,* Man That Stands Ahead, or Stands First, by his people.

So he returned across the portage and told the unhappy father that he need sorrow no more. And he stood among the assembled Indians and told them what he had found, and that he was sure that the children had escaped the Red Enemy. Gitchie Meegwon, holding in his hands the scorched and blackened top of the basket, only wished he knew.

That night, after camp had been made and it had fallen dark, Big Feather climbed a great, bare, rocky hill that stood high above the face of the Wilderness, and there, with the wrecked and ruined forest stretching out on every side below him, his face painted in dark lines of sorrow, he raised his arms towards the sky and prayed aloud to the Great Spirit of the Wild Lands:

"O-way! O-way! Manitou, O Spirit that watches over all the Forest People, keep my little ones from harm. Keep my children safe.

Since they have gone my days lie dead around my feet, as do the ashes of this burnt and broken Wilderness.

The Sun does not shine any more, and I cannot hear the Singing Birds. I hear only the laughing voice of Sajo; all I

* Pronounced Nee-*gan*-ik-*ab*-o.

BIG FEATHER STOOD
THERE IN THE MOONLIGHT

*see is the face of my Shapian with his brave eyes, facing the
flaming forest.*

*Manitou, I have done wrong. The fault is mine. I, who
brought sorrow to the heart of Sajo, cast a shadow across the
smiling face of Sajo.*

*O Gitchie Manitou, bring them safely back to O-pee-pee-
soway, The Place of Talking Waters. Great Spirit of our
people, keep my children safe.*

O-way-soam! O-way!"

And while his voice rang out across the empty, silent burnt
lands, there sat behind him in the moonlight, the old white-
haired Chief, with his wrinkled face and his eyes so full of
wisdom, who tapped slowly, and softly, on a painted drum.

Meanwhile Sajo and Shapian, all unknown to their anxious
father, were hastening, farther and farther away from the Land
of Talking Waters, speeding onwards through the darkness
towards the distant city, as fast as the hurrying wheels of a
train could take them.

XIII

The Little Prisoner

AND meanwhile what of Chikanee?

We must go back to the day the trader walked out of Gitchie Meegwon's camp with him, right out of the lives of his friends, it seemed, for ever.

During the four or five days it took the trader, with his Ojibway canoeman, to make the journey back to Rabbit Portage, Chikanee did not fare so badly, as one of the Indians took good care of him, keeping him well supplied with feed and water. But he could not understand why Chilawee was not with him, and wondered where Sajo and Shapian had disappeared to. And he began to be lonesome for them all, and often cried out for Sajo to come to him, as she had always done when she heard the little beaver calling. But no one came except the strange Indian, and then only to change his water and to give him food. This man, by the trader's orders, accompanied Chikanee on the steamboat to see that he arrived safely at the railroad, and there left him; the money for him was paid over to the Indian, and what happened to him now did not greatly matter.

Having now come to a stop, and thinking that he must be home again, he wailed loudly for liberty and recognition, expecting his playmates to come and take him out of this stuffy and uncomfortable box. But none came. So he started to chew at the box, and strange, harsh voices spoke angrily to him. He next tried to climb the walls of his prison, but they were too high, and these strangers shouted at him, and pounded on the box to keep him quiet, and now, thoroughly frightened, he lay still, whimpering and lonely. Where, oh, where was Sajo, who had always comforted him in his small troubles, and in whose arms he had so often found such happiness? Where was Chilawee, from whom he had never before been separated for so much as an hour?

A little later he was loaded onto a train that thundered and roared its way for many hours. When the train first started, he forgot to close his ears, as a beaver can do to keep out water and unpleasant sounds. The noise drove him nearly crazy, and in his terror he tried to dive to freedom through his tiny dish of water, and upset it; so that besides his other misery he soon began to suffer from thirst. He had been snatched away from home too hurriedly for Sajo to have time to drop a bannock in the box, which would have lasted him several days, and no one thought of providing him with anything to eat, and now, sick, hungry, lonesome, and wild with fear, he started desperately to cut his way out of the crate. In this he would have quickly succeeded, but striking a nail he broke one of his four cutting teeth, which made gnawing too painful to continue. His bedding, what little there was of it, became dirty, and the motion of the train thumped and bumped him against the hard sides of the box, so that he became bruised and sore. He tried hard to stay in the center, away from the walls of his prison, but never could. One of the trainmen, intending to be kind, threw to him some crusts of bread from his own lunch, but he thought that the little beaver's frantic clutchings at his hands was a sign of ill-temper. Chickanee was just a wild animal to these people, who did not know that he only wanted to be helped, and from then on they were afraid of him—so small a creature to be afraid of!—and no one attempted to give him any more bedding or food, and his water dish remained empty for the same reason.

And he raised his voice in cries of misery and called and called for his small companions, who now could never hear him, wailed in his childlike voice for them to come and take away this great trouble that had befallen him. But no one paid any attention, if they ever even heard him, drowned as was his feeble outcry by the uproar of the train.

At length, after many stops and starts, each of which jolted and slammed him from one hard side of his prison to the other, and a last, and cruelly rough ride in a delivery bus, there came a sudden quietness. The cleats were taken from across the top of the box with a frightful screeching as the nails were drawn, and he was lifted out by a hand that held him very firmly by the tail; a large, strong hand, yet somehow a very gentle one. Then the other hand came up and was held against his chest as he hung head down, bringing him right end up, and a finger rubbed gently on one hot, tired little paw, and a deep voice spoke soothing words; so that suddenly he felt rather comfortable. For this man was a keeper of animals, and attendant in the park where Chikanee was to stay, and he knew his business very well. And when he examined his small captive, and saw how miserable, and bedraggled, and covered with dirt the little creature was—he who had been so proud and careful of his coat!—the keeper said angrily to the delivery man, who, poor fellow, was not to blame at all:

"No water, nothing to eat, dry feet, dry tail, dry nose, teeth all broken up; if that isn't a shame, nothing ever was! Some way to ship a beaver, I'll say! But we'll soon fix you up, old-timer." For the man had been expecting his little guest, having had a letter about him, and had everything ready to receive him. Chikanee soon found himself in an enclosure built of something like stone, but not nearly as friendly as stone, and surrounded by a rail of iron bars.

And in this jail of iron and concrete Chikanee, for no crime at all, was to spend the rest of his days. Chikanee, gentle, lovable Chikanee, was now supposed to be a wild and probably dangerous beast!

It was not a very large place, a mere hutch after the freedom of the big lake beside which he had spent most of his short life, but that did not matter for the moment—he smelled water! And then he saw, right in front of him, a deep, clear pool; not a very big one, to be sure, but at least it was water. Into this he immediately threw himself and drank thirstily, floating on the surface, while the cracked and dried-out tail and feet soaked up the life-giving moisture, and the cakes of dirt loosened and washed from off him as he swam slowly back and forth. This seemed like the beaver's heaven itself, after more than three days of noise, starvation, dirt, and utter misery, and the hot, fevered little body cooled off and all the bumps and bruises ceased to throb, as the cool water slowly got in its good work on him.

And now, he thought, this must be just the plunge-hole. Down there, somewhere, lay the entrance, and through this he would set out and would, no doubt, come to his home-lake, there to find his playmates on the shore; and then Chilawee would run to welcome him and roll on his woolly back with joy, and Sajo would come and pick him up, and hug him and make much of him, and whisper in his ear, and tickle him in that funny place under his chin, and all these hard times would be forgotten.

So, with a great splurge he dived straight down—to strike his head on the hard bottom of the pool, almost stunning himself. Again he tried, with the same result. He scratched and bit at the concrete, thinking to tear his way through it to the tunnel that must, somewhere, lead out of it. But he only cracked and split his claws and took more chips out of his remaining teeth. Then he scrambled out of the pool and over to the bars, and tried to squeeze through them; but they were too close together. He tried to gnaw at them, but his broken teeth never even scratched them. So he ran round and round inside the enclosure, stopping here and there to dig, but to no purpose. For a long time he worked, running back to the pool and out again to the bars, trying to gnaw, trying to dig; but it was useless. At last he realized that there was no opening anywhere, no plunge-hole, no escape; and weary, wretched and hopeless, he lay flat on the hard, hot floor of the pen and

IN THIS JAIL OF IRON AND CONCRETE, FOR
NO CRIME AT ALL, HE WAS TO SPEND THE
REST OF HIS DAYS

moaned, moaned as he had done when Sajo had nursed him to sleep whenever he had been lonesome—only then he had moaned with joy, and now it was from misery. And his little paws ached for just one touch of Chilawee's soft, silky fur. And now there was no Sajo, no Chilawee, only one unhappy Little Small in prison, all alone.

The attendant stood by for a long time, and watched and shook his head, and said, "Too bad, little fellow, too bad." This was his job, taming these wild creatures that were sent to him from time to time; yet, liking animals as he did, he sometimes hated the work. To him they often seemed to be, not wild things at all, but hopeless, unfortunate little people who could not speak, and who sometimes were so pitifully in need of the kindness for which they could not ask; and he had always felt that a man, who was so much bigger and stronger, and knew so many things that they did not, should be good to them and help them all he could. He pitied the little beaver that was struggling so helplessly to be free, for this was not the first one that had come under his care, and he knew their gentle nature. And stepping in through the gate of the pen, he picked up Chikanee carefully and cleverly, so that, as in the first place, he was not scared or excited, but was actually comfortable in his hands—they were so much more friendly than the concrete!

The keeper carried Chikanee to his cottage, which was close by, inside the park. He had three young children, and when they saw their father bringing in a little beaver, they crowded round to see, and they shouted and clapped their hands with glee, so that Chikanee was afraid again, and tried to burrow into the man's coat; for already he had begun to trust him. And their father quieted the young ones and set the little creature on the floor where, finding himself once more in a house, he felt a little more at home than in the cage. They all stood watching to see what he would do, and the keeper's wife said:

"The wee mite! Look how thin he is. Joey,"—to one of the youngsters—"go get an apple; those other beavers we used to have were just crazy for apples."

So this Joey fellow went and got one right away, and put it down on the floor in front of Chikanee. He had never seen an apple before, but he sniffed at it and oh, what a wonderful smell came from it! And so he cut into it as best he could with his poor broken teeth and then, what a taste!—the most delicious taste in all the world! And seizing hold of this so wonderful tidbit with both hands, he demolished nearly the half of it. At this the keeper was very pleased, for some of his prisoners refused all food and died, but now he knew that this one would recover; something he had been none too sure about. And the delighted children laughed to see him sitting up there like a little man while he ate, and the keeper's wife exclaimed:

"There, didn't I tell you? He'll be all right in no time."

Then the man brought in the sprays of fresh, juicy poplar leaves he had placed in the pen for Chikanee, but which he had not touched. But now he ate them, and the children wondered to see him holding the leaves in little bunches in his hands while he put them in his mouth. Feeling a good deal better, by now, he made small sounds of pleasure while he ate, and at that the young ones marvelled even more, and one, a little girl with golden hair and a round, rosy face, said:

"Listen, listen to him talk, just like a little, wee baby. Oh, daddy, do let's keep him in the kitchen!" And their mother spoke up, too: "Yes, Alec, let's keep him here for a spell; there's no one in the park—it's almost like putting a child in prison." And Alec answered:

"Perhaps you're right. We'll fix him a place in here for to-night."

So they made a place for our Chikanee in the kitchen, and Alec the keeper fastened a low, wide pan of water to the floor, and set a large box down on its side, with plenty of clean straw in it for a bed for him. And there the little beaver spent the night, not happily, perhaps, but very comfortably.

The next morning Alec returned him to the pen, so that any of the public who came to the park could see him; but when evening came round again and the grounds were empty, the keeper brought him back to the cottage. And from then on he did this every day, and Chikanee spent all the hours when he was not "working," in the keeper's house, and in the kitchen had his bed, and his big pan of water, and ate his leaves and twigs there. Each day he had a nice, juicy apple, which quite made up for a lot of his troubles, though not for all of them; for never would he be anything but lonesome, so long as he lived.* Every morning there was a considerable mess to clean up, of peeled sticks, and cut branches, and left-over leaves, and

---

* Beavers possess probably the longest memory of any North American animal, much resembling the elephant in this respect.

the floor was all slopped up with water, but the children willingly turned to and cleaned up, after the beaver was carried away to his daily task of being stared at in the cage. Nobody seemed to mind the little trouble he was. He got along famously with the family and, in his own small way, soon became quite a part of the household.

As time went on he got to know them all. He would romp clumsily with the youngsters; and to them he was a kind of tumbling, good-natured toy, a good deal like one of those roguish wool puppies to be found on Christmas trees. But to Chikanee, it could never be the same as it had been at O-pee-pee-soway, and often he didn't want to play, but lay quietly in his box, his little heart filled with a great, empty longing for his old playmates.

Before very long his teeth had grown in, and he spent a lot of time sharpening them against one another, grinding and rattling them together at a great rate. A beaver's teeth grow continuously and he grinds and sharpens them constantly. His coat, which he had sadly neglected for a time, so that it had become all tangled and awry, now got its daily scrubbing and combing, and his small frame, that had for a while been little more than a bag of bones, soon filled out, and he began to look like the old Chikanee again. In a way he was happy; but never quite.

While in the cage he was really miserable, and the keeper knew this, and always felt badly when he put the little fellow in there each morning, and looked back at this pitiful little creature that gazed after him so wistfully as he walked away, sitting there alone on the bare cement floor, surrounded by bars that would have held a grizzly bear. He remembered that a beaver may live more than twenty years—twenty years in that prison of iron and concrete! In twenty years his own family would be grown up and away from there; he himself might be gone. The town would have become a great city (it was not really a very big place); people would come and go—free people, happy people—and through it all, this unhappy little beast, who had done no harm to any one, and seemed only to want some one to be kind to him, would, for twenty long and lonely years, look out through the bars of that wretched pen as though he had been some violent criminal; waiting for the freedom that would never be his, waiting only to die at last. And, thought the keeper, for no good reason at all, except that a few thoughtless people, who did not really care if they ever saw a beaver, might stare for a minute or two at the disconsolate little prisoner, and then go away and forget they had ever seen him. Somehow it did not seem fair, to this kind-hearted man, and when he watched the little creature rollicking with the children in his funny, clumsy way, he wished very much that there was something that he could do about it, and decided to make his small prisoner as happy as he could, and give him the freedom of the cottage as long as it was at all possible.

But Chikanee had not quite given up; he had one hope that for a long time he never lost. He quite expected that, in some mysterious way, Chilawee would come to join him; for in the old days, no matter where he had happened to be, it had not been long before Chilawee had turned up, looking for him.

And so, every so often he searched for him very carefully, looking in the wooden hut that stood in the enclosure, going patiently all through the downstairs rooms of the cottage, sometimes taking a run outside and examining the woodshed very thoroughly, very sure that some day he would find him. But after a whole month of daily disappointments he began to lose courage, and at last gave up his search that always turned out to be such a failure.

And hundreds of miles away, Chilawee was doing the very same thing, and all for nothing.

Chikanee was just beginning to get over this, when something took place that was the very worst of all—and yet something that was very near to his dearest wish. One day an Indian woman, with a bright shawl on her head, passed by the pen. The moment he saw her, Chikanee dashed wildly at the bars, reached through them with clutching paws, and let out a piercing cry, for fear she would pass him by. At this the woman stopped and spoke to him, and the sounds she made were the same as he had heard so often in the Indian country, at home! But not the voice. And seeing her face, and catching the scent of her, he turned and plodded slowly back to the bare wooden hut again, more dejected and downcast than he had ever been. He had thought it was Sajo.

But this experience stirred him, and brought new hopes to him; he got the idea that some day Sajo *would* come. And from then on he watched for her. Crowds of people visited the park in the afternoons, and most of them paused by his cage to see what a beaver was like. But his "customers" never stayed long, and soon passed on; to most of them he looked to be just a scrubby little pup with a flat tail. Some just gazed carelessly, others curiously, a few poked sticks at him and made harsh and, as he thought, threatening sounds; a few, a very few pitied him, and one or two were friendly and gave him peanuts and candy —but none of them was Sajo. But he continued to hope, and spent his time watching closely every face he saw, sniffing every hand he could get near to. But he never saw the face he looked for, never caught the scent of that so-beloved little hand. Yet he was sure that some day a well-remembered voice would call out, "Chik-a-*nee!*" that the small brown hands whose touch had so often thrilled his little body, would again pick him up, and then —oh! the joy of once more pushing his nose close into that special spot in a certain warm, soft neck, there to puff and blow a little while and then to slumber, and forget!

Hours at a time he spent this way, watching, waiting, hoping; and later, on his little pallet in the kitchen, he would think, in some dim and misty way, of the happy days that seemed now to have been so long ago, and thought of the little chamber under Shapian's bed, that Chilawee and he had had between them for their very own, and of the crazy, tiny beaver house, and all the other arrangements that they had worked so bravely at together. And at last he became listless, and kept to himself, even when he was supposed to be happy in the kitchen; and he never played with the children any more. He neglected his coat, so that it became matted and unkempt. And he began to refuse his food, and would sit with his apple untouched in his hands, his little head drooping, eyes closed, breathing fast and heavily.

And the keeper, looking at him sorrowfully, knew that there was no longer any need to worry about the twenty years; or any years.

Chikanee wasn't going to live.

And the wee brain grew hot and feverish with longing, and he seemed sometimes almost to see his old playfellows there before him, and thinking of them fell asleep, and sleeping dreamed of them. For animals *do* dream, as perhaps you know, and often wake up half scared to pieces from a nightmare, just as you or I do, and from the sounds they sometimes make, some of their dreams must be quite pleasant, too.

One evening he awoke from a dream that was so real, that he thought himself once more at home with his friends, so he got up and ran whimpering about the kitchen, looking for them, and not finding them cried out again and again in loud sobbing wails, from very lonesomeness and misery. And as he cried, his voice was like the voice of a small, lost child.

For he did not, could not know, that less than a mile away, in another and similar room, was another and similar little beaver, and that there with him, waiting for morning, too excited to even think of sleeping, were two little Indians—a boy that stood straight and proudly, like an arrow, and a little girl who wore a brightly coloured head-shawl.

And in one corner of the room there stood an old familiar, well-worn, birch-bark basket.

Yes, you guessed it. Sajo and Shapian had really come, at last.

XIV

Patrick the Policeman

WHEN the train on which Sajo, Shapian, and their small
fellow-traveller Chilawee, were riding, made the last of
its many stops and came to a standstill in the city station, the
children were almost too scared to get off. The conductor, who
had had his eye on them all the way, helped them out, spoke a
few words of encouragement, and left them to attend to his
other duties.

They found themselves in a world of noise. The hurrying
throngs of people, the hiss of escaping steam, the clang of engine
bells, the shriek of whistles and the thunderous bellowing of
starting and stopping locomotives, deafened and terrified them,
and they stood hand in hand on the platform, not knowing
which way to turn and not daring to move. Before, behind,
and on every side of them was a terrific confusion and a ceaseless din. Lorries piled high with baggage of every kind rumbled
by, and one of these came straight for them and Shapian pulled
his sister aside only just in time to escape being run over by it.
The depot was, to them, a vast, echoing cave filled with terrify-
ing sights and sounds, and never before had they felt so small
and defenceless. They felt more alone here, in the midst of all
these people, than they had ever done in the forest, with its
silence and its quiet, peaceful trees. People looked at them
curiously as they passed, but every one seemed to be too busy

rushing this way and that to pay much attention to them.

So there they stood, in all that deafening uproar, two little people from the Silent Places, as scared and bewildered, and nearly as helpless, as the two tiny kitten beavers had been when Gitchie Meegwon found them floating on the Yellow Birch river. Yet Sajo, with all her fear, had only one thought—Chikanee had come through all this *alone!* While Shapian began to wish himself back in the forest fire again, amongst the friendly animals. Chilawee, for his part, closed his ears as tightly as two tiny black purses and lay perfectly still, jammed into a corner of his basket.

They had been standing there for what seemed to them an hour (though it had really been only a few moments), and Shapian was thinking of making *some* kind of a move towards a huge door through which crowds of people were flowing like a swift, rushing river, when there stopped in front of them a young boy. He was about Shapian's own age, and was dressed in a neat, red uniform with bright buttons all down the front of his short, tightly fitting coat. On the side of his head there was a little hat that looked more like a very small, round box than anything else.

"Hullo, you kids," he said cheerfully, "are you lost? Who are you looking for?"

Poor Shapian, confronted by this self-possessed and magnificent-looking personage, and never before having seen a page boy, found that he had completely forgotten any English he ever knew. He could remember only one word; so he said it.

"Poliss-man," he stammered nervously.

"You want a policeman, eh?" said the page, who was a smart lad and got to the point at once. "Come along with me." And beckoning to them he set off at a great pace, his shiny boot-heels tapping sharply on the hard platform. The little Indians, silent-footed in their moccasins, slipped softly along behind him, though they nearly had to trot to keep up, Shapian carrying Chilawee's basket in one hand and holding tightly to his sister with the other. It must have been a queer-looking procession! Their guide steered them through the crowds, over to the entrance and down a great hall filled with more people, nearly all the people in the world, thought Shapian, and brought them over to a big, stout man who stood beside a door at the far end. He also had a number of bright buttons on his coat.

"Hey, Pat," the page called to him, "here's a couple of kids want to see a policeman," and pushed them forward, continuing, rather disrespectfully, I fear, "You shouldn't be hard to see, you're big enough. Look like Indians to me—better watch your scalp!" And with an impudent grin at the police officer and a wink at the children, he dodged into the crowd and disappeared.

"Oho," exclaimed the policeman loudly, looking down on the two youngsters, with his hands behind his back, "Oho, so it's scalps, is it?" said he, looking very fiercely at them, as though he were about to take them prisoner—though his eyes had an odd twinkle about them and were pleasantly crinkled at the corners. " 'Tis young Injuns yez are, eh? The little craytures! Well, 'tis a mighty poor scalp ye'll get from me, that's been bald as an egg this twenty years; and well did the little imp know it that brought ye here!"

He was built something on the lines of Father Christmas, and although he talked so fiercely his face was round and jolly, and he wore his helmet a little to one side of his head in rather a jaunty sort of fashion, as though being a policeman was the most entertaining business imaginable. But seeing that the "little craytures" were becoming alarmed, he asked, in what he considered to be a lower voice (I don't think he had any low voice, myself):

"And what can I be doin' for ye?"

"You—poliss-man?" asked Shapian timidly.

"Yes, me lad," answered the constable, putting his helmet just a trifle more to one side, "I'm a policeman, and a good one —the O'Reillys have iver been of the best—Hullo! what's in the basket?" For Chilawee had now commenced to wail.

"A-mik," answered Shapian, taking off the lid for him to see and repeated "A-mik," at which, to his great astonishment, the policeman began to laugh very loud indeed, "Ho-hoho-hoho! so it's a Mick he calls me, knew I was Irish right away—sharp as a di'mond, the little haythen. Ye said it me boy, I'm a Mick, sure I'm a Mick." For he was very proud indeed of being Irish, and imagined that Shapian had known it when he used the Indian word "A-mik," which means, of course, "Beaver." He thought this Indian lad very smart to have discovered it; and Shapian, hearing him say so often that he was "a Mick," came to the conclusion that he belonged to some strange race of white men who called themselves "Beavers," a very honourable title indeed! And so, finding such extremely good points in one another, each of them found the other to be a rather clever

"Oho!" said the policeman "So its scalps, isit?"

fellow, which put them at once on the very best of terms.

"And where would ye be wantin' to go?" now asked the policeman.

Shapian, along with his English, had quite forgotten the letter Yellow Hair had given him, but now remembering one, he thought of the other, and pulling it out gave it to the officer, who read the address on the envelope and said,

"I see. I'm on dooty and cannot leave; but set ye down and wait, and I'll take ye there. And it's Patrick O'Reilly himself will see that no harm comes to yez." And he patted Sajo kindly on the head, and Shapian having at last been able to tell him in English what Chilawee really was, he asked to see him, and pronounced him to be a "fine little baste, what there was of him," as he didn't see a great deal, for our bold Chilawee had become very meek indeed, probably thinking by the way things were going that the end of the world had come, and he hid his head, and his tail, and all his legs and feet and made himself as small, and as he thought, as invisible as possible, and certainly he was not much to look at, for the time being at least.

And so our two young wanderers, feeling a good deal more at their ease, sat on the end of a long row of seats and waited. And the big policeman, who seemed to be in such continual good humour over nothing at all, asked them a number of questions, and Shapian, having got his English into pretty fair working order by now, told him most of the story. And the jolly Irishman became quite depressed about it, and said that he— Patrick O'Reilly himself, mind you—would take them to the people who owned the park, "And it's meself as will tell them the plain truth, with both hands, so I will," he said aloud, and so disturbed did the worthy officer become as he thought the matter over, that he got a little mixed in his speech. " 'Twould bring tears to the eyes of a heart of stone," he declared. "Melt the candles off a Christmas tree, so it would!"

A little later he was relieved by another constable, who joked good-naturedly with him about the "family" he had got for himself, and they then went out together onto the street, where there were fewer people, and there was not so much bustle and noise. Their new friend talked nearly the whole time, for he was doing his very best to make them feel at home, and Shapian talked too, in his queer, broken English. Sajo listened meanwhile, all eyes and ears, though she could not understand anything; but she felt that they were safe with this big, blue-coated man beside them and now no longer afraid, she felt like crying out with happiness; for was not Chikanee right here, in this very city, perhaps on this self-same street? And she began to enjoy looking around at the wonders that were to be seen on every side—horses, which she had heard about but never seen before, the street-cars that sailed along so nicely without even a horse to draw them, beautiful ladies in beautiful clothes, and best of all, the gay shop windows. Once they passed a restaurant, and the smell of food and the sight of the delicious-looking pies and cakes in the window brought their weary little faces round so sharply in that direction, that the policeman, noticing it, and hearing them whisper together in Indian, guessed that they were hungry.

"Well, now," he exclaimed, "and it's hungry yez are, and me

blatherin' away like some ould gossip, with the two of yez near
ready to drop, belike. 'Tis not the way of the O'Reillys to
l'ave a friend shtarvin' to death on the doorstep, so to spake.
We'll in and have a bite."

"Yessplease," said Shapian. "My sister, that's hungry long
time now," though it would have been hard to say which of
them was the hungrier. So Patrick herded them into the place
ahead of him, and after they were seated he asked them when
they had eaten last, and Shapian told him,

"At trading post. Me, I have not that fear; but my sister,
now, have plenty. So sit down all time one place, eat nothing.
Me, I take care my sister. That's never leave him alone, my
sister. So nobody eat, only little bit Chilawee his bannock."
And the policeman said,

"Ye're a brave lad. The O'Reillys, now—" But we are
doomed never to hear just what the O'Reillys would have done
about the matter, for at this moment the waiter came in with
their order, and the children's eyes grew round as doorknobs,
and very nearly as big, when they saw the tray piled high with
cheerfully steaming eatables. These looked so tantalizing, and
smelled so delicious, that when the dishes were set before them
the children were quite overpowered. Sajo even felt a little
faint, so excited was she, and soon they were too well occupied
to talk, look, or listen, or to do anything else but eat, and
eat; and there was some wonderfully fast work done around
that table in the next few minutes. And while they were enjoying themselves, Sajo remembered that poor Chilawee must be
hungry too, and she put tidbits from her plate into the basket,

of bread and butter, and doughnuts, and pie and I don't know what all, and soon he was as busy as the rest of them, making up for a whole lot of lost time.

They were in one of those small private dining rooms that most restaurants have, and they were all by themselves, and now that the feast was pretty well over and nobody, not even Chilawee, could possibly have eaten one more mouthful, everybody sat back and began to feel exceedingly comfortable. Mr. O'Reilly lit a cigar, and being, if possible, in even better humour than before, beamed around on his guests in a state of the highest satisfaction. His helmet was off, and Shapian, being no longer busy, now had time to see that he was not quite so bald as he had claimed to be—bald as an egg, he had said—for a wide ring of hair started just above one of his ears and worked back, and around, till it came to the other ear; quite a respectable amount of hair, considering, far more than you will find on even the very best of eggs!

Sajo, like the good little housekeeper she was, piled all the dishes neatly away to one side, finding it great fun to handle these rich-looking things, although they were really nothing more than ordinary china tableware; but she, poor child, had never *seen* such dishes, as she told Shapian that night.

It was warm in the small room, and Sajo put back her bright head-shawl, showing her long, shining black braids and her soft, dark eyes, all alight with happiness just now, and the officer, who now saw her face properly for the first time, said she was the prettiest little girl he had ever seen since he'd "left Ireland, where they have the finest-lookin' gurrls in the wurrld!"

And Shapian told her what he had said, and she blushed and
hung her head, and pulled the head-shawl up again. But no
one could be shy very long with this good-natured man, and she
soon got over it and looked up at him, so that her shawl slipped
back again, and this time she left it there, and she laughed at
all the things he was saying although she couldn't understand
a word of it. Shapian, glad to see his sister so light-hearted,
laughed nearly as much as she. And Officer O'Reilly, mighty
pleased at the success of his little party, laughed so heartily that
he was obliged to open his coat, and mop his bald spot with a
large red handkerchief that he pulled out of his sleeve; and
taking it all around, they were all in uncommonly high spirits.
Even Chilawee was heard from, and he and Sajo had a little
private conversation of their own, while Mr. O'Reilly tried his
hand at learning to talk Indian from Shapian. I'm afraid he
didn't make very much progress; but there is one word that
Indians use very often, "kaeget," which means "certainly," or
"sure," or "indeed," and if you are *very* sure, you say "kae-*get*."
Now this was easy to say, and Pat caught on to it very soon, and
when Shapian told him what it meant, he practised it until he
had it right. From then on it was kae-*get* this, and kae-*get*
that, and he was very proud indeed of his new word. And so
he explained the plans he had made for the next day, talking,
as nearly as he could, in Shapian's broken English:

"That park," he said, following Shapian's own style, "That
park, closed." Here he closed the door of the room, very firmly.
"Tomorrow, open park, give money, beaver come!" And opening wide the door, threw out his arm like a "go-ahead" traffic

signal and stood aside, as though he expected a whole troop of beavers to come marching in through the opening. Then he brought out the letter, and tapping it said,

"Me, come this place. Tomorrow. You wait." And, with another flourish of the signal, "Kay-*get*."

Shapian, whose English was not quite as bad as all that, found it hard to keep from smiling, understood very well, and said so, and the good Mr. O'Reilly was very pleased with his first lesson in Indian, and really felt that he began to understand something of the language.

He saw his "family" safely to their address, and turned them and the letter over to the manager of the place, making sure they understood that he would be back for them in the morning, telling them on no account to move until he came. The manager seemed to be expecting them; in fact, he had already received a telegram about them, and as soon as he had put them safely away for the night, he sent away a telegram himself. And at the same time, in his own modest home, Pat the policeman was holding a long conversation over the telephone about them; also, up at the distant fur post at Rabbit Portage, there was a considerable stir taking place on their account. And altogether, there was quite a fuss going on over these three little wanderers—a fuss about which they knew nothing whatever.

Upstairs, the two children talked excitedly, but in whispers, for somehow this grand, white-walled chamber gave them a feeling of being very small and out of place, like two mice that had stolen into somebody's pantry, or into a church.

But it was a place where no accidents could ever happen,

that was certain, so in the safety of this room, Shapian took out their little wad of money from a deerskin pouch that hung from a string about his neck. He spread it out and smoothed each bill very carefully on the table, while Sajo looked on, and nodded her shiny black head as if to say, "There you are, that's what my dream did!" They tried to make out just how much there was, Sajo standing by with her finger on her lips and her head on one side, looking very wise, while Shapian frowned and wondered, and looked closely at each bill; but the figures didn't mean a thing to them, and they had to give it up. But anyway, there was plenty, they agreed, more money than they had ever seen before; and Shapian folded it all up again and put it back into its little bag, under his shirt.

For this was the price of Chikanee's freedom and must never, for one single moment, be out of reach.

Meanwhile Chilawee, on the floor, was having the time of his life in the wash dish. He was having, at the same time, another feast, from a loaf of bread which the manager had kindly supplied, and what part of it he had not been able to eat, was slowly being transformed into a mushy, gooey, sticky mess, and you can take my word for it that the rug on which all this was taking place, was in no way improved by the performance.

Not one of them could sleep. The little beaver because there were far too many interesting things to be found under the bed, and in the clothes closet, and in corners, and the children because tomorrow was to be that great, that wonderful day of days, for which they had worked so hard and gone through so many dangers, and for which they had waited so long.

Tomorrow they would actually have Chikanee!

And neither one of them ever stopped to think that the park people might refuse, that they might never let the little beaver go, now that they had him. For, whatever misgivings Shapian may perhaps have had, Sajo, sure that her dream was coming true, never once doubted, and only said:

"Tomorrow we have Chikanee. I *know*."

XV

Unto the Least of These

Early the following day, Patrick O'Reilly called for his charges, as he had promised. But they did not go right away to the animal park as they had expected, but to a large building in the city, where the park owners had an office.

Afraid that at the last moment, some accident might happen to the money, Shapian felt often at the lump under his shirt, where the little bag was; they were going to need it very soon now, and he was getting nervous. In the other hand he carried Chilawee in his basket and beside him, never more than three feet away, Sajo walked with short, little-girl steps, her shawl wrapped about her head and shoulders.

There was a swift ride in an elevator, which they far from enjoyed, and then they found themselves, with the Irishman beside them, standing before a desk behind which sat a man.

And this was the man in whose hands was the fate of their little lost friend.

Sajo, who up till now had had such faith in her dream, became suddenly fearful and anxious, and trembled like a leaf. She had no idea what they were going to do if their offer was refused; and now that the moment had arrived she wanted to scream and run away. But she stood her ground bravely, determined to see it through, no matter what happened.

The man behind the desk was a youngish man with a pale narrow face and a weak-looking chin. He had a cigarette in the corner of his mouth, burnt almost down to his lips, and one of his eyes was screwed up unpleasantly, to keep the smoke out of it, while he looked around with the other, so that at times he appeared cross-eyed. He spoke without removing the cigarette, squinting sharply at them with the eye that was in working order; and a very colourless, unfriendly-looking eye it was.

"Well, what do you want?" he asked shortly.

There was a moment's silence, a very heavy, thick kind of a silence. I think that Sajo and Shapian had even stopped breathing. Then:

"Sorr," commenced Pat the policeman, "I telephoned Mr. H—— last night concerning me young friends there, and we were all to meet him here, to talk over a shmall matter of business, belike——"

"You can do your business with me," broke in the young man, in no very civil tone. "Mr. H—— is busy at present." And he glanced towards a door that led into another room, and which stood slightly open.

"You see, 'tis this way," began Pat once more, when the young man looked at his wrist watch and interrupted again.

"Make it snappy, constable; I'm busy this morning."

Pat got a little red in the face and again started his speech, this time successfully. It was a speech that he had carefully rehearsed the night before, the story that, as he had said at the railroad station, was going to "bring tears to the eyes of a heart of stone." Evidently the young man did not have a heart of stone, however, for there were no tears; in fact, while

Pat was talking, this impatient personage looked several times at his wrist watch, and lit a fresh cigarette from the stump in his mouth. Far from having a heart of stone, it began to look very much as though he had no heart at all. And the honest policeman became a little discouraged towards the last, and finished his tale rather lamely:

". . . so the young people wants to buy the little baste back from ye: and I'll be so bold as to say that I think ye'll be doin' the Lord's own wurrk if ye let them have it." And having done his best he stood there, nervously wiping his face with the big red handkerchief. The man straightened some papers on the desk and leaned back in his chair.

"Are you quite done?" he inquired coldly.

"Yes," answered Pat, none too happily, for he began to fear, and with good reason, that he had lost the battle already.

"Oh," said the clerk, "thank you. Well, let me tell you"— his words fell like chips of ice on a plate of glass—"that beaver was bought in a fair and perfectly businesslike way, and not from these ragamuffins at all, but from a reputable trader. We paid fifty dollars for him, which was a great deal more than the little brute was worth, and we have no intention of selling him back—unless we can get a good profit on the deal, and" —here he looked at the two little Indians—"I don't think by their looks your red-skinned *friends,* as you call them, are very well off anyway."

Pat turned redder than ever, but shrewdly suspecting that money alone could talk to this hard-headed fellow, he pushed Shapian forward.

"Money," he whispered hoarsely. "That money. Money, give it now!" And Shapian, sick with fear, for he had understood nearly everything, stepped forward, fumbled for a moment in the pouch, and dropped his little wad of money on the desk.

The clerk took it, counted it. He sniffed.

"There's only fourteen dollars here." He handed it back. "Nothing doing!" he said, and to make sure that everybody understood, he added, for good measure, "All washed up; no sale; no good; no! Get me?"

They got him; every one of them.

Nobody spoke, nobody moved; but to Shapian it was the end of the world—but no—was this true? And then the silence seemed suddenly to be choking him; the white face of the man behind the desk was getting bigger and bigger, was rushing towards him—the floor seemed to be going from under his feet—was he going to fall like a woman, faint like a girl! He closed his eyes to shut out the sight of that pale, weak face with its one eye that leered at him so mockingly; he gritted his teeth, clenched his fists, and stiffened his young body upright in his old, proud way; and the dizzy feeling passed, leaving him cold and trembling. Meanwhile the policeman stood helplessly by in his dismay, mopping his bald head and mumbling huskily, "Oh, the shame it is! The pity of it! And it's me that's betrayed them that trusted in me; 'twill bring sorrow to the ould heart of me for many's the day!"

And Sajo? She had been watching every move with painful eagerness, her eyes flitting from face to face like two frightened birds in a cage; and she had seen. No one needed to tell her.

They had failed. In just two minutes they had failed.

She came softly over beside Shapian. "I know, my brother," she said very quietly, in such a strange little voice that Shapian looked at her quickly, and put his arm about her, while she stood close, looking up at him, "I know now. He is not going to give us Chikanee. I was wrong—about my dream. We have come to the city not to get Chikanee, after all. I think—per-haps—it was—to bring Chilawee to him. That must be what my mother meant; so they could be together—so they won't be lonesome any more. That must be it. So——"

And her childish voice fell to a whisper, and the little dark head drooped. "Tell this man—I—give him—Chilawee—too."

And she set Chilawee's basket upon the desk and stepped back, her face like a sheet of paper, her lips pale, and her eyes wide and dry, staring at the basket.

O'Reilly, cutting short his lament, stood aghast; *now* what was going on?

"What's this," exclaimed the clerk, becoming angry. And Shapian told him: " 'Nother beaver, Chilawee. His brother, that Chikanee, very lonesome. You keep him Chilawee too; not be lonesome then. Those are words of my sister. Me—" his voice stuck in his throat, and he couldn't say any more.

"Well, now," said the clerk, smiling for the first time, though the smile improved his face very little. "That's a horse of a different colour! We'll fix that up very quickly," and he reached for his pen——

"NO!!" suddenly shouted the policeman in a terrific voice,

bringing his fist down on the desk with a crash, so that every-body jumped, and the ink bottles and paperweights and the pens and the pencils all jumped. And even the pale young man jumped and turned a shade paler, and his cigarette jumped from his lips to the floor.

"No, you don't," bellowed Pat in a tremendous voice. "No son of an O'Reilly will stand by and see a couple of helpless kids bullyragged and put upon by ye, nor the likes o' ye. Ye're a black-hearted scoundrel!" he roared, "an' I'm an officer of the law, an' I'll arrest ye for conspiracy, an' fraud, an' mis-demeanour, an' highway robbery, an' assault, an'—" Here he ran out of the more attractive-sounding crimes, and growling fiercely started round the desk towards the badly scared young man, who was backing away as hastily as possible in the direc-tion of the other room, while Sajo and Shapian stood by with eyes as big as saucers. Just what this rather violent son of the O'Reillys intended to do, never became known, for at that moment the other door opened, and the fleeing young man found his line of retreat cut off, as he stumbled backwards into yet another guest to the party, and a voice, a very quiet, low voice said: "Pardon me," as there appeared just inside the room a slim, grey-haired old gentleman, who stood peering over his spectacles at this astonishing scene.

He gave a slight cough, and said again: "Pardon me, if I appear to intrude," and then invited, very politely, "Won't you sit down?"

Pat still snorted angrily and glared at his intended prisoner, who was not at all sure if he *hadn't* committed some crime or another, so that his hands trembled a little as he fumbled with a new cigarette.

"Pray sit down, gentlemen," again invited the grey-haired man.

They sat down; somehow you felt that you must do as this mild-mannered old gentleman asked you. And he it was that owned the park; it was Mr. H—— himself.

"Now, let us talk matters over," he suggested, looking from the policeman to the clerk, then to the children, and back to the policeman again. "Now, constable, on the telephone last night I promised to hear these children's story, and to consider what should be done. I have heard everything—from the other room, far better than if I had been here; for then certain things *did* happen, that would not otherwise have done so. I had already learned from you how far they have come, and what hardships and dangers they have been through to try and regain their pet. But I had to be careful; I had to know that it was not a fraud, and as I cannot understand their language, I wanted to see what they would do, before I could even consider the matter. Now I know the *whole* story, and I see that matters are going to be very difficult—for me."

At this, the clerk looked around with a pleased expression, as if to say, "There now, didn't I tell you?" Mr. H—— looked around too, tapping his spectacles on his knee:

"Every one is listening, I hope?" he continued. "Yes?" It was plain to be seen that he was very well used to having people listen to him; and he held his glasses, which were of the pince-nez variety, across the thin bridge of his nose with his thumb and forefinger, and peered through them at each in turn, and the children found his gaze to be rather piercing, quite different from his voice.

"Ah," he said, finding that everybody was waiting to hear more (although Sajo did not understand a word he said, she was fascinated by his queer mannerisms and the smooth, even flowing of his speech). "Very good. Now, I heard these Indian children offer to give up their other pet, so the two little animals could be together, which proves to me their truthfulness. But, there is my side to be thought of. As George, here, says, it was a perfectly proper piece of business, and it cost me quite a sum of money. I cannot decide all at once. Moreover, it is not good for people, especially young people, for them to have everything they ask for, not, that is, unless they have worked for it." And he looked at them a trifle severely through his glasses, which he had put on again.

"And what are ye figurin' to do, Sorr?" asked O'Reilly anxiously, wishing that he would stop fidgeting with his spectacles and get down to business. But Mr. H—— turned to his clerk: "You are a good business man, George, almost too good, I sometimes think."

"I was only doing my duty, Sir," answered George, with some truth.

"Ah, our duty; yes," mused the thoughtful Mr. H——. "Well, no matter."

"But what are ye goin' to do about it, Sorr?" again asked Pat, nearly exploding with impatience.

"Do?" queried this exasperating old man. "Do? Oh, yes;

I think I have decided what to do—just this!" and taking Chilawee's basket he beckoned the children over. "There," he said gently. "There is your small friend. Now," and becoming all at once very brisk and businesslike, he wrote something on a card and handed it to Pat. "And now, go down to the park with Mr. O'Reilly, *and get the other one*. He is yours; you most certainly have earned him."

Shapian stared, his mouth open—did he hear aright? Or was this another one of Sajo's dreams in which he had become entangled? Or perhaps it was one of his own! But Sajo was very much awake, and she grabbed Chilawee's basket from him.

"Tell me, *tell* me," she clamoured excitedly, "what is it, what *is* it?" And seeing that they did not quite understand, Mr. H—— was about to speak again, when Pat burst out (he so wanted to be the first with the good news!).

"Pardon me, Sorr, I speak their langwidge," and he turned to Shapian: "Him," he said, giving Mr. H—— several good hearty slaps on the back, so that gentleman, caught unawares, almost went forward on his face, and his glasses went flying (much to every one's relief), "that's good feller. Him"—here he gave the astonished Mr. H—— a sound thump on the chest that nearly bowled him over backwards—"him, that's big chief, good. Me—'tis a difficult tongue, Sorr—you, catchem two beavers, chop, chop. Savvy?" And finishing in his very best Indian "Kaeget! Kae*get!*" he turned triumphantly to Mr. H—— "Langwidges was always a gift with the O'Reillys, Sorr."

"Quite," said Mr. H——. "Most decidedly—ah—yes!" And he smiled as he let the happy party out through the door, and closed it behind them, still smiling gently to himself. What an extremely pleasant little game it had been, he thought, even if he was, after all, the loser! And he rubbed his hands together very cheerfully, quite as though he had made rather a profitable bargain.

I greatly doubt if either Sajo or Shapian remembered very much about that trip to the amusement park, up to the time that Pat pointed out the entrance that could now be seen not far ahead of them. Then Sajo started to run. She was not pale now, and her eyes, that had been so dry and staring, were all aglow. Her shawl fell back unheeded, and her braids flew out and bobbed up and down on her shoulders, as her little moccasined feet pattered on the pavement. Behind her came Shapian, unable to keep up with her on account of carrying the basket, inside which Chilawee, tired of being cooped up for so long, was making a great uproar. Next came the stalwart Mr. O'Reilly, very red in the face, his helmet off, dabbing with his large red handkerchief at the head that had been "bald as an egg for twenty years," puffing and blowing like a tugboat that had a light touch of asthma.

Once he bellowed "Hey! What is this, a race?" But the youngsters kept right on going, and it is very doubtful if they ever heard him; so he fell to grumbling: "The little haythens, they'll be the death of me yet, so they will." But he kept valiantly on.

Several passers-by stopped to look at the young Indians in

their forest clothes, racing along the street with the policeman apparently chasing them. They heard, too, the shrill cries and wails coming out of the basket, as Chilawee objected loudly to the shaking up he was getting in all this hurry; so a few of them turned and joined this strange parade, and followed this small, running, black-haired girl.

And behind them all, far, far behind, there came another person, a tall, brown-skinned man who strode along so softly, yet so swiftly through the city streets. And he looked so dark and stern that people were glad to step aside and let him pass, and stared after him and said to one another: "Who is that? What kind of a man is that?" But he never so much as glanced at any one of them.

There was some delay at the entrance, as the park was not yet open for the day, but O'Reilly soon caught up, and showed his card, and they were let in. Quite a respectable crowd had gathered, and pushed in with them as soon as the gates were opened. The attendant, who was none other than our friend Alec the keeper, already knew what to do, as Mr. H—— had decided, at the last moment, to come too, and had given his orders and now stood in the crowd. At a nod from Mr. H—— the keeper led Sajo quickly over towards the beaver pen. And all at once she was pale as a ghost again. She seemed to be running in a great empty space at the end of which, miles away, was a dark, ugly looking row of iron bars, and now, now—she could see through them, and there—yes, there was a brown, furry little animal sitting up in the center of them, and was it?—could it be?—yes, it was—Chikanee!!

And Sajo, no longer shy, forgot the watching people, forgot the noisy city, forgot everything but the small furry body that was now so close, and rushing to the iron fence she threw herself on her knees in the gravel, thrust her two arms through the bars, and screamed: "Chikanee! CHIKANEE!! CHIKA-NEE!!!"

The little beaver, not believing, sat without a move, looking.

"It's me, Sajo; O! Chikanee!" The cry was almost a wail: Oh, had he forgotten?

For a moment longer the little creature stood there, stock still, his chubby brown head cocked to one side, listening, as Sajo cried out again:

"Chik-a-*nee-e-e-e!!!*"—and then he knew. And with a funny little noise in his throat, he scrambled as fast as his short legs would carry him, to the bars.

At that a little cheer broke out amongst the crowd, and there was a small commotion. Alec the keeper now came forward and opened a small iron gate, and said: "This way Miss —a—Mam'selle—a—Señorita—" for he didn't quite know how he should address her, and was rather excited himself. And she rushed in, and kneeling down gathered the so-long-lost Chikanee up on her lap and bent over him; and they both were very still. And the gay head-shawl hid everything; and neither you, nor I, nor any one else will ever know just what passed between those two on that fateful, that glorious, that never-to-be-forgotten morning.

And the grey-haired Mr. H—— took his handkerchief from his pocket and blew his nose rather loudly, and Alec the keeper had suddenly become troubled with a cough; "Humph," he said. "Hurrumph."

"You bet!" exclaimed Pat the policeman in a hearty voice, although the keeper hadn't really said anything at all.

And now was to come the biggest thrill of all. Chilawee and Chikanee were to have *their* party now. They were only ten feet apart, and didn't know it! What a thrill was there!

So it was with wildly beating heart that Sajo and Shapian carried the basket in; one of them alone could never have handled this affair; it took the two of them to pull off the lid, they were in such a state. And they lifted Chilawee out, and set him down facing Chikanee, a short distance away. Then they stood and watched, breathlessly. For a second or two neither of the kittens moved, just stared at each other. Then, the truth slowly dawning in the little twilight minds, they crept towards one another, eyes almost starting out of their heads, ears wide open, listening, sniffing, creeping slowly forward until the creep became a walk, and the walk became a little shuffling trot, and now, sure at last that they had found each other, the trot broke suddenly into a gallop and with a rush they met, head-on. And so violent was the collision, in a mild way of speaking, that, not being able to go any farther ahead, they went straight up on end, and with loud shrill cries they grasped each other tightly and there, in front of all those people, began to wrestle!

The ceaseless, hopeless searching, the daily disappointments, all the misery and longing, the dreary, empty nights of lonesomeness were over.

Big Small and Little Small were together again.

Before long they were disporting themselves all over the enclosure, and what had been a grim and ugly prison, had now become a playground, the best use that it had ever yet been put to, I'll guarantee! And the children clapped their hands, and shouted, and laughed and hallooed at them excitedly, while the wrestlers, or dancers, or whatever you have a mind to call them, stepped around in high feather, enjoying to the utmost what must have been to them the greatest moment in all their lives, up to that time and perhaps for ever after. Never before had they given quite such a brilliant performance; and the people cheered them on, and laughed, and the grey-haired Mr. H—— waved his handkerchief quite furiously in the air, and I am not at all sure that he didn't shout a little himself.

Mr. O'Reilly, just about dying to take a part in this happy occasion which he had helped so much to bring about, and very proud to think that he was the only one present who knew the whole story, appointed himself Master of Ceremonies, and while he performed his duties as a policeman and kept back the crowd, he also played the part of a modern radio announcer, and explained to them what it was all about, and cracked jokes, and beamed around on everybody in the most amiable fashion, and otherwise enjoyed himself immensely. And I think we will all agree that he was entitled to any credit he got, even if he did pretend to know a little more about it than he really did. And when the two Smalls commenced to do their queer-looking dance, he was not to be outdone, and was heard to say that it was the very first time in all his days that he had ever seen anything but an Irishman able to dance a good Irish jig; and he ended up by declaring for all to hear:

"AND THERE, BEFORE ALL THOSE PEOPLE,
THEY BEGAN TO WRESTLE"

"Well, I'm seein' it, but, be japers, I'll never believe it."

For which he could have been very easily excused as, to any one who had never seen such a thing before, it must have been a most extraordinary sight.

And then, having been there, watching, for quite some time, for he had not wished to interrupt this little celebration, there now came out from behind the people another figure—a tall, dark man in moccasins. He was the same man who, a short time before, had been seen striding so swiftly through the city streets in this direction. A quietness fell upon the wondering crowd as he stepped forward. Sajo and Shapian, busy with their playfellows, never noticed him until a voice, *the* voice, the one they knew so very well, said softly there behind them, in the quiet, musical language of the Ojibways:

"O-way, the clouds have indeed gone from off the face of the sun. Now my sorrow has gone too, melted away like the mists of early morning. These people have done much, very much for us, my children. Let us thank them.

"My son, my daughter, take up your Nitchie-keewense,* your Little Brothers.   O-pee-pee-soway is waiting."

Big Feather had come to take them, all four of them, back to The Place of Talking Waters, to the Land of the North West Wind.

And Sajo's dream had, after all, come true.

* Pronounced *Nit*-chie-*kee*-wense.

XVI

Mino–ta–kiyah!

So they bid farewell to the city, with its noise and its bustle and its people who, after all, thought Sajo, seemed to be just about the same as any other folks—more good ones than bad ones. In fact, nearly all good ones, she decided, and made up her mind to tell the Indians just what they really *were* like.

And they said good-bye to Alec the keeper, who had been so kind to poor, lonely Chikanee, and who felt very relieved to see his little prisoner free once more; and to the whimsical, quietly smiling Mr. H——, who was happy for a long time after, in the knowledge that he had brought gladness to some very sorrowful hearts. Although Gitchie Meegwon had tried to pay him for Chikanee, he would not even hear of it, and said that it was worth the pleasure it had given him.

Patrick the policeman, stalwart son of the O'Reillys, brought them to the railroad station and saw them off; as he told his comrades afterwards, "Wid me own two hands I saw thim safely on their way. And whin their fayther heard me sp'akin' his langwidge to the youngsters, he smiled all over his face, so he did!" Which it is quite likely that he did. And as the train pulled out from the platform, the two children waved and waved to this friend who had been so good, and loyal, and true to them, and he stood there holding his helmet high in the air like a signal, his bald pate shining in the distance, leaving Shapian still firmly convinced that there was a whole nation of people living on a green island in a great salt lake, who called themselves Beavers.

When they arrived at Rabbit Portage, the first person they saw was Yellow Hair, who jumped aboard the boat before it was well landed, to welcome them. Right away, Shapian gave him the money that was left, and Yellow Hair told the Big Knives, who were all there to meet them, and offered it back to them. But one of them stepped out and made a little speech, and said that they were all very glad that things had turned out so well, and that the missionary was to keep the money and give it to some one amongst the Indians who might be poor, and needed it. And Gitchie Meegwon thanked them all for their kindness to his children, and said he hoped that some day it would come *his* turn to help some one, as your turn always came around some time, to do a good deed.

Yellow Hair told them that he was to accompany them back to the village, where he was going to work among the people. And at this the trader, who up till now had kept rather in the background, came forward and shook hands with all three of them and said that he was coming too, so that he could become better acquainted with his Indian customers, as all good traders should; though he never mentioned, never *would* mention, never *did* mention, that he too had helped. And it never would have been known if Yellow Hair had not seen him that time in the schoolhouse, and told Big Feather about it privately. Meanwhile, the two Smalls came in for a great deal of petting and attention, and they even consented to stage a wrestling bout for the assembled Gitchie Mokoman, though I doubt very much if they cared whether anybody saw them or not; and I think they were rather relieved when the party set out and they were left in their basket to themselves.

Big Feather paddled in his own canoe, which still showed the effects of the fire, and Shapian took the bow. Sajo, on this trip, did no work but was a passenger, along with Chilawee and Chikanee who never worked anyway, and she sat with her face stuck into the beaver box most of the time. Yellow Hair and the trader went with some more Indians in another and much larger canoe, one of those great birch-bark canoes called Rabi-shaws, with a high, proudly curving bow and stern, which gave it rather the appearance of some gallant charger, or a Spanish galleon.

At the first portage they found the old Chief, Stands First, encamped, awaiting them. He asked for an account of all that had happened, and listened very attentively as they told him, and at all the important points and especially interesting places, he said "Hoh!" and "Hah!" and "Hum!" in a deep, throaty voice, and there was a very knowing twinkle in his eye as he listened. After considering the matter for a while, he told Sajo and Shapian that they were an honour to their people, and that there would be a song made about them, and about their adventures with the Little Talking Brothers, as he called the Smalls, and that it would become a part of the history of the tribe. And he looked in on Chilawee and Chikanee and said that they too now belonged to the tribe, and would become a great tradition in the nation. And as he spoke there was a smile on his wise old wrinkled face, the first that had been there for many a long day; for he was rather a grim-looking old man, to tell the truth. And then, pulling his blanket about his waist he stood there very straight, with his long white hair about his shoulders, and made a sign with his hand towards the sun and said,

"Hah! Mino-ta-kiyah; kae*get* kee mino-ta-kiyah!—it is well, indeed, it is very well!"

And all the watching group of Indians, and Gitchie Meegwon, and Yellow Hair, repeated together like a chorus, "Mino-ta-kiyah!" and everybody seemed to be very solemn and impressed.

And as they journeyed on their way, on to O-pee-pee-soway, the trees beside the river seemed to wave to one another and to nod, and in the rustling of their branches and their leaves, they seemed to sigh "Kaeget mino-ta-kiyah, it is well"; the ravens in the air croaked "Mino-ta-kiyah!"* and the wind whispered through the grasses, "Se-e-e-e-ey mino-ta-kiyah"; and the racing water in the rapids, that once had seemed to be so fierce and wild, sang it over and over in that strange way that running water has; and the little swirling eddies that slipped from off the paddles, murmured it at every stroke, "Mino-ta-kiyah."

Never had the forest seemed more beautiful, never had the sky been quite so blue; and the sun had never shone so brightly, nor the squirrels frisked as gaily nor the birds sung half so

---

* Pronounced Mee-*no*-tak-*kiy*-ah.

sweetly, as they did for Sajo, on that journey back to O-pee-pee-soway. And never had she or Shapian, in all their lives, been quite so happy.

When they arrived, Big Feather called all the people together, and at his cabin that night they held a dance of celebration. Everybody from the village came, including two or three half-breeds who were passing through (and who had *not* bothered anybody's hunting ground after all) and who, as usual, had their fiddles with them. And there were swift, clever step-dances while the fiddlers played old-time jigs and reels, the players putting into the tunes all kinds of queer twists and turns, after the fashion of the half-breeds; and there were Indian quadrilles with as many as twenty people on the floor at once. And the fun was fast and furious.

All the boys of the village wanted to dance with Sajo, so that she was kept pretty busy, and I can tell you, by the way, that she was quite a little dancer, for I myself was there and saw her, and saw Shapian, too, who was as proud as Punch to see his sister so much in demand. You may be sure that he had no trouble in finding dancing partners among the village maidens, and there were some very fine-looking young women to choose from, as could be plainly seen, because there was no ducking and hiding behind head-shawls, for none but the oldest ladies would ever think of wearing one to an affair of this kind.

Outside, a huge fire was kept burning, where tea was constantly being made, and before which had gathered a little group of old men who sat and smoked, and talked of olden days, whilst a crowd of youngsters played tag, and hide and seek among the flickering shadows. And Gitchie Meegwon passed among his guests, and talked with them, and his face, that was sometimes stern and often sad, was now very pleasant to look at as he smiled upon them all and bid them welcome. Every once in a while he went around with a large pail of tea, while Sajo and Shapian carried cups and served the people, and danced in between times.

Once during the evening the dancers cleared the floor, and sat back in a big circle against the wall as though expecting something to take place, and a hush fell on them. Soon two drummers took their place inside the circle with tom-toms, and commenced to beat. And then, through the door, came old Ne-Ganik-Abo, Stands First, the Chief, with a great bonnet of eagle feathers on his head and strange, wild-looking designs of paint upon his face, and danced to the sound of the drums. Below each of his knees there hung a circlet of hollow deer hoofs, that clinked and clanked at every step, and in his hand he held a rattle made of a whole turtle shell, painted red and black, and having the head and neck of the turtle for a handle. And as he danced, the hollow deer-hoofs fairly rang, like little copper bells, keeping time with the swift movements of his feet, and the fringes of his buckskins quivered and shook, and the great bonnet nodded, and opened wide across his shoulders, and closed and spread again, all in perfect time with the drums, which never stopped beating, and he shook his rattle very fiercely as he danced. And while he danced, he sang a low, weird chant, in which he told the adventures of Sajo and Shapian, and of Chilawee and Chikanee, as in the old days when the warriors had sung the story of a battle. And after each verse there was a chorus, given by a group of singers; and the song had a queer haunting melody that was somehow very exciting.

This was the song he had promised, and it would now be one of the legends of the tribe; for it was by means of such songs about various happenings, and by crudely painted pictures of events, that the old-time Indians kept a record of the history of their people. But the trader, who had never seen such goings on before and thought it was a war-dance, became the least bit alarmed, until Gitchie Meegwon explained to him that it was not a war-dance at all, but a Wabeno,* used only by the Medicine Men, or for the reciting of great events. Then with one loud, long yell the Wabeno came to an end.

And now the fiddles struck up a lively tune, and the floor filled up and the fun commenced where it had left off, and away went the quadrilles and the jigs again. Yellow Hair danced on nimble feet, and laughed the whole night through, and picked the homeliest old woman he could find for a partner; and when things slackened down for any length of time, he got them going again in very short order. And the trader, surrounded by all the merry throng, quite forgot his dignity, and let it be plainly seen that he could be just as jolly as the next man, and made no bones about it either, but footed it as merrily as the best of them. He even made friends with the Smalls, but still could never remember their names, though Shapian, who didn't hate him any more, did his best to tell him. But he kept

* Pronounced *waw*-beno.

"NE-GANIK-ABO DANCED TO THE SOUND OF THE DRUMS, AS THE WARRIORS HAD DONE IN ANCIENT DAYS."

on calling them Chilakee, and Cherokee, and Chikaroo and any number of other names that sounded something the same, but were always wrong, and of which he seemed to have an unlimited supply.

Chilawee and Chikanee themselves were by no means left out of things. They never would be left out of anything so long as they had two voices to shout with, and four legs apiece to run around on, and excited as they were by the music and the noise and all the fun, they tore about the floor, and scrambled between the dancers, and went around begging wherever they could find any one sitting down. Once Chilawee took the center of the room and stood there upright, fair and square in the people's way, and the dance had to be stopped in that particular set, because nobody wanted to trample on the little fellow, or fall over him. For a minute or two he had it all to himself, and held the floor, so to speak, and stood looking around as if to say, like Long John Silver: "Here I am, and here I stay, and you may lay to *that*." So Sajo finally had to carry the young ruffian bodily off the floor, kicking and squealing. Meanwhile Chikanee (the saint!), who had lived in the city and knew a thing or two, had found out where there was a case of apples that some one had brought up from the trading post, and discovering that one apple was about all he could cram into himself, he started carrying them away one by one and hiding them, and when he was found and arrested there was a real circus and another squealing match. Hoping to quiet them down, Sajo began giving them chunks of bannock to go to bed with. But they would not stay there and came bobbing out for more, so they were continually running back and forth with these bribes; and it is very certain that even if they had stuffed themselves all night, they could not possibly have eaten the half of it.

At last, tired out with the long journey, and the excitement, and this and that, and one thing and another, they finally retired to their own private chamber for good; and with their noses tight together, their little hands clutched in each other's fur, and entirely surrounded by bannock, they drifted off to sleep, all their troubles, all the long, weary days of lonesomeness, gone forever and forgotten.

From then on, all day and every day, the play-house and the lake shore rang with shouting and with laughter, as they had done before Chikanee had ever gone away. It began to seem as if such a thing had never really happened, but had been nothing but an ugly dream. The cabin, that for so many days had stood empty and forlorn, was once more filled with joy. And the soft ground at the landing bore again the print of little feet whose owners, those with two feet as well as those with four, had come so near to leaving no more footprints, ever, anywhere.

Chilawee, the scapegrace, became once again the bold, bad pirate, and was as wilful as he had ever been, or a little worse, if you ask me. He disappeared as regularly as ever, and could be depended on to be found just as regularly, and always up to some mischief or another, and when caught at it would do his absurd, wigglesome dance and fall on his back with a great outcry, either from delight at his prank, or just out of sheer naughtiness. Although they were both beginning to be quite a size by now, Chikanee had given up the race to see who could grow the fastest, and he had allowed Chilawee to get a little ahead of him. And there he stayed, so that Chikanee was still the Littlest Small and was as soft and gentle in his ways as he had ever been. Not that he was good *all* the time; that would have been too much to expect. But many and many was the time when he lay in Sajo's arms, as in the old days, with his nose pushed tight as could be against her throat in just one certain spot that he knew of. And there he would snuggle up, and close his eyes, and puff and blow a little, and make small whimpers of happiness, just as he had done so often in his dreams on his lonely little pallet in the keeper's kitchen. And now he was never to be lonely any more—and he would open one eye and take a look, to make quite sure that he was still there and that it was not just another of those dreams!

And now everything was the same as ever, and the days were very full, and busy, and exciting, with all the swimming and the burrowing, the puddling in the mud and the combing and scrubbing of coats, and the games of hide and seek under the canoe, and the wrestling and the amateur building operations on the tiny, crazy beaver house that just never *could* keep out the rain. And then, after all the work and the play was over for the day, the short, weary legs plodded up the water trail to the cabin; and there were the little dishes (the same little dishes!) full of boiled rice, or milk, or, on special occasions, even a little dash of preserves, and then a good stout chunk of bannock apiece to go to bed with, and the long sleep on a soft, warm bed——

And so the happy Summer passed.

Came the Autumn, and with it the Days of Falling Leaves, the Silent Days. The time had come to take Chilawee and Chikanee back to their old home. For they must now be allowed to take up again the life that was rightly theirs, and follow the way of all the Beaver People. In the Winter it would be impossible to supply them with enough water for their needs, nor could they be moved from place to place, as in the Summer. And Gitchie Meegwon called his children to him one day, and explained it all to them very carefully, and told them how the beavers, who would soon begin to grow up, could not much longer remain happily living in such an unnatural way, and that very soon they must be returned to their own folk, to live as the Great Spirit of the Wilderness had intended they should.

The children had known for some time that this must be so, though they had never mentioned it to one another. As the day for the parting drew near, Sajo became very quiet and thoughtful, and spent long hours with her small play-fellows, who would soon be hers no longer; while they, merry as a pair of sand-boys, played with her in the same old frolicsome way, with never a thought for the days to come, even though they should be happy ones.

And she loved them so much that she would not think of how lonesome *she* might be after they were gone, but of how glad *they* would be to see their father and their mother once again. So how can I be sad? she asked herself, and then said aloud, in rather a quavery little voice,

"I'm very happy. I *am*. I *know* I am!" So there!

Yes, Sajo, you were happy; happy as must be, always, those who give.

And so, one morning in October, in the Month of Falling Leaves, when the hills were all crimson, and brown, and golden in their Autumn colours, Chikanee and Chilawee, Little Small and Big Small, took their leave of their little private room and the cabin where they had spent the happy, carefree days of kittenhood. And they left the shaky little beaver lodge, and the play-house, and the water trail and all their landing places, left them there behind them on the shore, and climbed into their old birch-bark basket that had served them so well and for so long, and embarked on the last and most important journey they had ever made.

And little did they guess, as they settled themselves down on their scented sweet-grass beds, how great an event was waiting for them at the other end of it.

XVII

In the Moon of Falling Leaves

I T was to be a big affair.

Sajo was gay in many-coloured tartan plaid, her newest, brightest head-shawl and her beautifully beaded moccasins. Shapian and Gitchie Meegwon had on their very best deerskin clothes, worn only on very special occasions, and newly smoked to a rich, velvety brown. On the famous basket Sajo had painted leaves and many-coloured flowers, and birds and little animals, to be company for Chilawee and Chikanee on this the last of all the journeys they would ever take in it; and with a big white feather hanging from the handle, and all the painted pictures, it looked no longer old, but like a new one. In it, with loving care, she had arranged a bed of sweet-scented grasses, and had tied to it, in a little leather bag all decorated with porcupine quills, the two small, but very precious dishes.

The canoe, that had carried them so staunchly and so well, and had shared so many of their adventures, had by no means been overlooked. No signs of the fire were left upon it. Its sides had been dyed a bright yellow, as before, and it had newly painted gunwales and a new eye, not so fierce as the one it had lost—rather a jolly-looking eye, come to look at it, and also a fine new tail. And a very proud appearance it made, as though it knew very well that this was to be no ordinary voyage; and out in the wind it wagged its new tail in a very frisky way indeed, and the eye, as the reeds and rushes blinked and nodded past it, seemed to be winking to itself as though its owner was very pleased about something or another.

And so they headed for the River of Yellow Birches, that lay far away in the blue distance among the Hills of the Whispering Leaves, where Chikanee and Chilawee had been born.

For six days they journeyed on. And ever, as they went, the air grew more still, the waters calmer. Every night long strings and lines of wild-geese flew overhead towards the South, the beat of their wings sounding very plainly in the darkness. Each morning the sun seemed a little larger and redder, the leaves more brilliant in their colouring. For the forest, in the days of Indian Summer, in the Moon of Falling Leaves, is very beautiful.

Sajo was really, truly happy; not at all as she had expected to feel. To keep herself that way, she kept remembering that her small, so-well-beloved friends, her Little Brothers, were going to be better off than they ever had been, and would soon be getting better care than she could ever give them—that they were going home, home amongst their own folks. Their play-days were almost over, she knew; they were becoming more sober-minded. Soon they would be going to work, as all the forest animals and nearly every kind of people must do sooner or later; that, she agreed (did you ever notice how easy it is to agree with yourself?), was what they were made for, not just to be pets, but to work; which was quite true. It was the only way that they could ever be really contented.

Yet there would come, once in a while, a little ache in her

heart, and her eyes would get a little blurred and misty; but she would brush her hand across them quickly, and say to herself, "I'm just sorry for *me*. That's only being selfish. We must do what is best for *them*. That's how much I love them." And she would look bravely around at the trees and the lake, and peep into the basket, and tickle the funny, pursey ears, and think how lovely it would be if only she could just see what went on, and hear what they said to one another when they got inside the lodge.

If only their father and mother and the other little ones would come to meet them, so she could see them all together! And she hoped, oh! how she hoped, that no hunter would ever find them.

On the last night of the journey, they camped amongst the pine trees in that pleasant spot where we first saw Gitchie Meegwon making his noon meal, so long ago, beside the little stream that came down from the beaver pond. And on this memorable night, after supper had been eaten and everything put away, and it was dark and the campfire was blazing away cheerfully, Big Feather said that he had something of importance to tell them, something that he had been keeping for the very last.

And everything settled down to be very quiet, as the children sat and listened there beside the glowing fire. And Chilawee, as he sat beside his basket, not moving at all, his head cocked to one side, beaver fashion, seemed to be listening; and Chikanee, lying with his head on Sajo's knee, quiet as a mouse, must have been listening too. The broad, deep river that flowed so silently and swiftly by, must certainly have heard it all, and no doubt repeated it over and over to the very first rapids that it came to. Even the great, dark trees that stood so solemnly and still around the camp, the shadows from the firelight flickering in and out between them, seemed to stand and listen as he spoke.

"Sajo, Shapian," said Gitchie Meegwon, "this is the last night we will spend with Chikanee and Chilawee. Tomorrow they will be back with their own people, to live in their own way. Very pleasant have been the days they spent with us. They have brought much joy to our house, and the bright days of Summer have been brighter because they came to us.

"I found them at this place, sick and helpless—dying. Now they are back here again, well and strong, ready to carry on. Their adventures are over, and they will be happy as never before.

"One thing I can promise; they will never be killed."

Here Sajo made a little sound, a very little sound, but she put her finger to her lips to push it back. Gitchie Meegwon went on:

"You saw our Chief dance the She-she-gwun, the Dance of Rattles; it was a Wabeno, for a special sign, and he has commanded that no Indian shall hunt beaver in or near this place. And here no white man ever comes. This is my hunting ground, but I myself will never harm them, or their family; it would be like killing small, friendly people. For they have made my children happy; could they understand me, I would thank them. Come what may, they will be forever safe.

"Tomorrow, when you let them go, I will give the call of a beaver, the sound with which they call to one another. The young ones in the lodge will not listen, but perhaps the old ones may come and greet them. I cannot be sure, but I will try."

Sajo put her hand tightly across her mouth, so there was no sound *this* time.* Just then a low moaning cry came floating out from somewhere in the hills, became louder for a while, and faded again to silence; a wild, deep-toned, yet lonesome wail—the cry of a wolf. Gitchie Meegwon paused until the last echo had died away, while every one listened; for Indians do not fear the wolves as some do, but look on them as fellow hunters, calling them The Lonely Ones. Then he continued:

"Big Small and Little Small," he smiled at the names, "will never be quite lost to you. Beavers are different from other animals; they are very like persons, and do not quickly change. Once they know you and have become your friends, they do not forget. They will be yours, always.

"And now the best thing of all" (no sound from anybody; not even the wolf). "Once every year, in the Moon of Falling Leaves, when the leaves of the forest are falling all about us like brightly painted red and yellow snowflakes, and the wild geese fly in clouds across the sky, then you shall come here, to their home, and stay a little time and watch beside their home-pond in the evenings, and see them swimming, working, playing. It is very likely that they may come to you, so you may speak to them, perhaps may even touch them. They may not be able to remember everything, and many of the things they saw with you may pass from their minds, but *you* they will

---

* Indians exercise great care to avoid interrupting when any one is speaking. On an occasion such as this, for a young person to speak, unless directly addressed, would be counted as a serious misdemeanour.

"THEY WILL NEVER FORGET YOU" SAID BIG FEATHER.

never forget. The old men, who are very wise, have told me. In my young days I, too, have seen it.

"My children, those are my words."

And they were words that took out from little Sajo's heart the last traces of sadness—not *quite* perhaps, for after all she was only a little girl, and she was giving up everything she had to give—these two tiny creatures that she loved as no one but a little girl *can* love. But they were not forgetful little people, her father had said, and, she thought, I will hang the basket on a tree, near the ground, and leave the little dishes too, where they can come and see them, so they *won't* forget. And that night, as she lay on her bed of balsam boughs, with Big Small and Little Small sleeping cuddled in her arms for the very last time, she thought over everything that had ever happened, since they had come to her on that never-to-be-forgotten birthday, and of all the good times they had had together, and how happily everything had turned out at the last, and she thought of everything that her father had said—he was going to call them, and maybe the old ones would come out, and everything—and it seemed a shame to sleep away this very last night of all. So she lay awake as long as she possibly could, listening to the quiet breathing of Chilawee and Chikanee, and at last she laid her little head, that was so full of thoughts, down beside the two small damp noses that puffed, and blew, and sometimes were inclined to snore, and soon she passed with them into the Land of Forgetfulness.

The next afternoon, just as the sun was setting, at the time when wild beavers awake from sleep, they were all beside the home-pond of the Beaver People. It was from here that Chikanee and Chilawee, two tiny, lost mites, had started out on their Great Adventure.

In most ways the place was much as it had been when we first saw it in May, the Month of Flowers. The dam was full and running over, and in the best of shape, and the earthen house still reared itself like a huge, dark mound, high above the fen-land. But the pond no longer looked to be deserted. Fresh work showed everywhere, making it appear more than ever as though a gang of men had been busy with axe and shovel. Yet all this was the work of two beavers, for the little ones do not count for much during their first Summer. The sides of the lodge had been all heavily plastered to keep out the cold, and floating out in front of it was an immense raft of logs, and sticks, and branches, which had been collected for the beavers' Winter food supply. From different places along the shore smooth, well-kept, narrow roads wound their way up into the woods, and alongside them a number of freshly cut stumps were visible, the very teeth marks plainly to be seen upon them. Most of the trees that had belonged to the stumps had disappeared, and were now hidden away under the raft, and a few others lay near the water partly cut into lengths, showing where the Beaver People were still at work, gathering in their harvest against the coming of Winter, which was soon to be upon them.

It was very quiet and peaceful there, and the ring of silent trees was reflected very clearly on the calm surface of the water, but their tops were no longer green, as they had been when we last saw them, but were red, and yellow, and brown, where the frost had painted them. And all around through the silent forest, the falling leaves came drifting, spinning, rustling slowly down.

Gitchie Meegwon drew away a short distance, while Sajo and Shapian carried the basket down to the water's edge between them. And there, beneath a tall, silvery poplar tree they opened it.

Shapian reached in and stroked the plump, silky little bodies, and said, "Farewell, Nitchie-kee-wense, good-bye, Little Brothers"; but not very loud, because his voice was a little shaky, and a man had to be careful about such things before the womenfolk. And then he took his sister's two hands in his own, and said to her:

"Do not sorrow, my sister. Every year when the leaves are falling, I will bring you here to see them. Many things have we four seen and done together; we will always remember, and *they* will not forget. Our father has said it. Now they will be happy, all their lives. It is well with them."

"Yes," Sajo answered in a whisper, "I know; they will be happy. So I must be happy, too." And she smiled up at him, "Thank you, my brother."

Then Shapian went over and stood with his father, and left Sajo there alone. She held the little beavers close, just for a moment, and whispered into the small black ears:

"Good-bye, Chilawee; good-bye, Chikanee, my Little Brothers. Don't let's forget—*ever*."

And then she let them go.

She followed them to the very edge of the water, where she stood watching them as they floated off. On they swam, on across their own home pond, their two round, chubby heads side by side, as they had always been; sturdy Chilawee, jovial, wayward and full of whims; gentle Chikanee, wistful, winsome and affectionate. A few more minutes and they would be gone. And no matter how big they might grow to be, in one tender, loving little heart they would still remain two tiny, helpless baby beavers.

To Sajo they would forever be the Smalls.

As they drew near to that great earthen stronghold across the way, Big Feather gave a long, clear call, the call of a beaver looking for his companions. Again the sound, like a note of music, stole out into the stillness; and again. And then, quite suddenly, a black head appeared on the surface of the water near the house, then another; great dark heads, with big furry brown bodies that floated high behind them.

Sajo scarcely breathed; it was just what she had hoped for, but had not dared to believe—the beaver father and mother were really coming, at Gitchie Meegwon's call, to meet them! Everything was coming true, *everything*— Oh!——

Every one stood as still as the trees themselves, while the old beavers came slowly towards Chikanee and Chilawee, passed around them once or twice, looking, sniffing at them, making some low, thrilling sounds, and then swam on beside them— big heads and little heads, all together now! Swimming steadily and swiftly on (oh, all too swiftly), they held on to their course, the water streaming out wide behind them in long, rippling V's; and once or twice there could be heard the faint, distant sound of childlike voices. The dark heads, the big ones still close beside the little ones, became smaller and smaller, farther and farther away, until, right before the entrance to the lodge, one by one, without a sound, they sank beneath the surface, out of sight.

Big Small and Little Small were home.

And Sajo stood there very still, like a many-coloured little statue, in her gay tartan dress and pretty moccasins, her headshawl fallen back and her glossy black braids shining in the glow of the setting sun. And so she remained, looking out over the little pond, with her red lips parted and her dark eyes bright and starry, watching until the last brown head was gone, and the very last ripple on the water had disappeared.

And just then, from among the golden, whispering leaves above her head, there came the rippling notes of a small, white-throated singing-bird. As the tiny feathered songster trilled his melody so joyously, his voice seemed to fill the quiet valley, and, to the ears of Sajo, he sang a message, of hope, of happiness, and love:

"Mino-ta-kiyah, it is well," he seemed to sing. "*Me*-me-me-e-e—*no*-no-no-o-o—*no*-ta-kiy—*no*-ta-kiy—*no*-ta-kiy—ah!"*

And Sajo, standing there so quietly among the falling leaves, her eyes still fixed eagerly on the dark mound that was the last

* The song of the white-throat or song sparrow, or Canada, resembles in both rhythm and sound the effect I have attempted to reproduce above. The white woodsmen translate his song "o-o-o—Can-a-da—Can-a-da—Can-a-da-ah," while the Indians claim he sings, "*Me*-me-me—*no*-ta-kiy—*no*-ta-kiy *no*-ta-kiy-*ah*." His

home of her Beaver People, repeated softly to herself, "Mee-no-ta-kiy-ah."

And the little basket, with its two wee dishes, its bed of scented grasses, and its gaily-painted animals and leaves and flowers, she hung upon a low branch near the ground, and left it there beside the clear, still water.

Then turning, with outstretched hands, and bravely smiling, she ran to meet her father and her brother.

.   .   .   .

And now the figures disappear and all are gone. Our journey is over; the tale is done.

While you have been listening to my story, the flickering fire in the center of the wigwam has burnt low, and only the gleaming coals remain. Behind us on the walls of skin our shadows fall big and dark.

We must go.

Yet sometimes, as you sit alone in the twilight of a Summer evening, and have nothing better to do, perhaps you may think of these two Indian children, who were real people, and had their fears and hopes, their troubles and their joys, very much the same as you yourself have; and think of Chilawee and Chikanee, two little beavers that loved them, and who really

plaintive, unfinished melody is to be heard everywhere in the North Woods during the summer months, and to many of us he stands, with the beaver and the pine tree, as symbolic of the wilderness. And because his song, to the Indian ear, echoes the reassuring phrase "It is well," to have one of these birds sing in a tree under which a person may be standing, is considered to be an omen of future happiness.

lived, and loved each other, and could be lonesome, and knew how to be happy too.

And so you may journey once more, in memory, to the Hills of the Whispering Leaves, and see again the tall dark pines that seem to nod and beckon as you pass them; and you may make another voyage in the yellow bark canoe, with its peering eye and its bravely flying tail.

And perhaps, too, you may hear, as you sit so quietly and still, the rustle of falling leaves, hear the magic call of Talking Waters, and the soft low sound of voices, the voices of the Forest People, both large and small, who dwell in that great, lone land that is so far away, that is so wild, and yet so beautiful, the Land of the North West Wind.

GLOSSARY OF OJIBWAY INDIAN WORDS

Comprised of common objects, etc., mentioned in the
narrative. Spelled phonetically, with meanings.

A-*coon*-amee — A dam.

Ag-wah-*nee*-win — Shawl (head shawl especially).

A-*jid*-a-mo — Squirrel ("head-downwards." Refers to a common attitude
of squirrel when clinging to a tree-trunk).

Am-*mik* — Beaver.

Am-*mik*-onse — Kitten beaver.

A-*nish*-an-*ab*-ay — An Indian.

*Ap*ta — A half.

Ap*to*-zaan — Noon (half of the day).

Ap*to*-zee — Half-breed.

Bash-ka-*jig*an — Gun, rifle.

Baw-*wat*-ik — Rapids; Falls — Gitchie Baw-*wat*-ik (generally '*Chie* Baw-
wat-ik).

Bish*u* — Lynx.

Buck-*kway*-jigan — Bread (bannock).

Bu-da-way — To make fire.

Bush-*quay*-gan — Buckskin. Any kind of hide that has been tanned.

Dow-E-*nin*-ee — Store-man (Trader).

E-*nin*-ee — Man.

E-*quay* — Woman.

E-*quay*-sance — Girl.

E-*Quee*-way-sance — Boy.

Git-chie — Big, great.

Git-chie *Mo*-ko-maan — Americans (Big Knives).

Gwee-*gwee*-shee — Whisky-jack (Whistler). A camp-bird.

Jee-maun — Canoe.

Jing-*go*-bee — Any kind of evergreen boughs, or brush.

Jing-*wat*ik — Pine tree.

Mae-*hing*-gen — Wolf.

Mah-*tig*-'*kiz*-zin — *Boot* (wooden moccasin).

Mee-gwon — Feather.

Mo-ko-maan — Knife.

Moose — Moose.

Muk-*ķiz*-zin — Moccasin.

Ne-*gan*-ik-*ab*-o — Man That Stands Ahead (Stands First).

Nee-*bah* — To sleep.

Nee-*bah*-gun — Tent.

Nee-*bay*-win — Bed.

Nee-beesh — Leaves.

Nee-beesh-*ab*-o — Tea (liquid leaves).

Nee-beesh-*abo*-gay — To make tea.

Nee-*giķ* (hard G.) — Otter.

Nee-min — To dance.

No-po-ming — The forest, wild lands.

O-*ho*-mis-see — Laughing owl. (Cree language.) Also *Wap*-a-ho.

O-*jeshķ* — Musk rat.

O-*nah*-gan — Dishes.

O-*nig*-gum — Portage.

O-pee-*pee*-soway — Place of Bubbling Water (Local dialect "Place of Talking Water").

Rab-a-shaw — Large Bark Canoe (generally twenty-two feet long. For freighting).

Sai-dee — Poplar tree.

Saķ-a-*hig*-gan — Lake.

Schķoo-day — Fire.

Schķoo-day-*jee*maun — Steamboat (Fire canoe).

Schķoo-day-o-*da*bah — Railroad train (Fire-sleigh).

Shag-a-nash — White person (particularly English-speaking).

Shee-sheeb — Duck.

Shong-*gwis*-see — Mink.

Sho-nia — Money.

Sug-*gus*-wah — To smoke.

Tig-a-wash — Box.

Ub-wee — Paddle.

*Wab*igon-ojeense — Mouse (Little-runner-in-the-clay).

Waw-bigon — Flower.

Wawb-*wey*-an — Blanket.

Waw-*goķ*-wet — Axe.

Waw-poose — Rabbit.

Waw-wash-*kay*-see — Deer.

Wig-wam — House, or *Tee*-pee. (Derived from Wigwas, meaning birch bark, as the Ojibway tee-pees are often made of sheets of birch bark.)

Wig-was — Birch bark.

Wig-was *Jee*-maun — Birch bark canoe.

Zak-a-tosh — Reeds and rushes (particularly bulrushes).

Zak-a-*tosh*-kah — Place of reeds and rushes.